CASSIE

Caroline Banks
Assistant Author Elizabeth Hall

Good Egg Publishing
Patent number 2361575

Good Egg Publishing

First publication 2005

© Copyright Caroline Banks and Elizabeth Hall 1998.

This book is sold subject to the conditions in accordance with the Copyright, Designs and Patents Act 1988.

All rights reserved.
No part of this publication may be reproduced or transmitted, in any form, or by any means, including printing, photocopying, recording, electronic and mechanical information storage/retrieval systems, without written permission from the publisher.

Published by
Good Egg Publishing,
21, Green End,
Great Brickhill,
Milton Keynes,
MK17 9AT.

01525 261865

ISBN 0-9549105-0-8

One of the illiterate poor.

Sarah

Born 19th May, 1872

CHAPTER 1

Sarah Atkins hung over the rubbing-board, breathing heavily. Her bloated belly pressed uncomfortably against the stone sink, alive with bubbling suds, eager for action. Damp wisps of fading, auburn hair clung to pained, sweated brow. Her distress obvious in the clenched, white knuckles that gripped the sodden garment.

Sarah's labour had begun. The tenth child pulsed for recognition, amid the steam, heat and toil of the building's laundry.

"As you have made your bed, so you will lie on it." Her mind slipped back to her mother's harsh sentence, many years ago, stamped upon her mind forever. The shamed, eight and a half months pregnant bride of a feckless, reluctant bridegroom; the black sheep of respectable greengrocers.

The desperate, widow, Isabelle Jameson had been forced to seek support from her two, Scottish brothers-in-law, Jock and Hamish Jameson, to bring the erring Sam Atkins to the altar. The two, shaggy-bearded, red-haired men from up yonder, in course-hewn kilts and feathered sporrans, put the fear of God into the arrogant Sam, turning his knees to jelly.

The repeated hiss, "Dinna ken?" through gritted teeth, the supercilious caressing of calf-slung daggers and feathered sporrans, brought the shaking, unwilling bridegroom, fearing for his vitals, so into line, that he would have wed anybody.

Sarah's labour continued, slowly, relentlessly, against the impetuous whistles, hoots and sirens of the awakened, murky

River Thames and noisy bustle of the laundry. The ancient, iron mangles clanked and groaned defiance at the insolence of impatient women. Merry chatter and raucous laughter, usually at the expense of their men-folk, vied with the tortuous wheeze of encrusted weave battling against numerous, rubbing boards. The nervous energy generated from Sarah's determination to finish the job, saturated the rough, sack apron, bravely trying to come to terms with the expanding figure. The wooden slats, paddled in water, held aloft her tiny feet and swollen ankles.

The buxom Alice Green observed the situation from the far side of the laundry. Copper stick in hand and billowing breasts, clamped in steel armour to the highest point that gravity would allow, she precariously lifted the last of the whites from the boiling, zinc copper into the blue rinse. The self acclaimed nurse and midwife knew that her services were needed. With a sniff and a business like pull of her cloth cap and a lift of the bosom with her forearms, she waddled over to Sarah's side.

"Come on gel that's enough, time yer went ter bed." Sarah, weary, let slip the sodden garment.

"Don't worry, we'll finish."

The women ceased their toil. A hushed silence crept over the place.

Cries of "Give 'em 'ere Alice." and "Shove 'em over." "Get ter bed gel," abounded. The unmistakable bond that men could never enter.

So it was, in a war-torn Britain, in nineteen fifteen, on a cold, blustery, March day, Cassie entered the harsh, yet distinct world of London's East End. Born into the unique, maritime, riverside hamlet of Shadwell, in the same, mean room and the same, wobbly knobbed, brass bed, as had all the others. Here too, she often received the unwelcome attention of her musically gifted but drink-bound husband.

Boy or girl, it mattered not, neither loved, nor unloved, just another mouth to feed and care for. All her desires and aspirations swallowed in the needs and wants of others.

Sarah stared at the stark, whitewashed, brick walls, the only relief, a large picture of Sir Walter Raleigh, enthusing enthralled youths with his exploits, "Go West Young Man."

What if she had gone with her first love? she mused.

The curtains flapped incessantly against the ever rattling window, straddling the chest-of-drawers that had seen better days. An iron cot, housing a much used teddy bear, stood bleakly on the far side. The chipped handle of a poe peeped, cheeky, from beneath the white-starched valance and bedraggled, patchwork counterpane.

She pondered upon the one child that God had taken from her, a ten month old boy. Yet, despite her many misgivings, was glad that he had spared her the rest.

The child whimpered in its warped shawl, Sarah drew the child dutifully to her breast. Its tiny fingers curled the warm soft flesh and the silky, red-downed head bobbed up and down with the exertions of its newly found need.

She gently smoothed the red down and prayed that, at forty-three, God would close her womb. The heavy tread of her husband striding over the outside landing added further force to her prayers. Sarah was God fearing.

Sam Atkins crossed the once brightly patterned lino and stood awkwardly on the multicoloured, heavy, rag rug at the bedside. In doing so, he clipped the spying handle of the poe and disdainfully toed it back under. He wouldn't be seen dead using one, despite the bog, as he called it, being way down at the far end of the landing. His large frame contrasted sharply with that of his wife's small form. A brightly coloured necktie knotted his thick neck, and a smell of strong shag oozed from his body. The black, boot polish brush had put a fine dark glaze over his white hair. Deep blue eyes flashed his wife. "So you've 'ad it then?"

She met his gaze but did not answer. Despite a shared bed, it would be an 'it,' until such times as he could bounce the little perisher upon his knee. At present, he wanted no part of it. Women's world and ways flummoxed him.

"Yer alright then?"

"Did you get the job?" she said, ignoring the last and rankling at the reason for his present plight.

"Well, on all accant."

All discussions and queries began with 'on all accant.'

"'E said, there might be a chance, but 'ees not sure."

"We've no need to be in this plight," she said accusingly.

"There yer go," he said, "on and on, on and on," his blustering turning to anger. "On and on," was his way of shutting her up. That she had reason, he'd never acknowledge, but each time, secretly, he vowed to drink less but there she was again, always trying to make him feel guilty.

"It'll be prison if those rates are not paid."

"Well, I ain't crawlin', and that's that."

Sarah saw no reason for cockneys to speak badly. She refused to tolerate such talk in her children; 'ain't, was a forbidden word but Sam despised the mealy m'athed wimps, frightened to dirty their 'ands and who spoke with plums in their m'aths.

A fortnight in prison cancelled the debt but the thought of it sent shivers down Sarah's spine. A law unto himself, it was true, but the children loved him and his music. Perhaps, she could get a flat to clean. Despite his bumptious attitude she knew in her heart that he was torn to pieces and finished, the best marine engineer in Shadwell.

Returning from a night's spree, his mate, Horace Crutcher, had slipped from the gangway and fallen into the river. Sam, a strong swimmer, had dived in to save his floundering friend, who, by this time had disappeared. In the dark and in a confused state, Sam retrieved a heavy, jute sack, under the mistaken belief that it was his mate. He was found on Wapping Stairs supporting the bundle, whilst poor Horace floated face down in the water. Sam was exonerated from any blame but, as he was supposed to be working instead of frolicking, the Shipping Company thought otherwise.

"I've a christening on Saturday, I'll pick up a bit there." He was referring to a jazz-band that he and his brothers had formed. They had given up on him long ago but he was still their brother and his musical talent was beyond dispute.

The arrival of the puffing Alice Green put an end to further conversation. The plump arms and uplifts were draped in purple cotton and the cap trimmed with a false roll of brown hair under the peak. She gave Sam the look of contempt that she gave all fathers, seeing them as the cause of all women's ills.

Sam returned the look. He wasn't going to be put down by any woman. Nevertheless, he knew that he didn't belong and withdrew, muttering dire threats under his breath. "A man can't be master in his own abode."

His usual talk of 'ee didn't know 'ow it 'appened,' cut no ice with her. One day, she decided to tell him, in no uncertain terms and without any decorum. Sam was truly shocked, as she had intended him to be. Sarah wouldn't have talked like that. It wasn't right in a woman. He'd never even heard Sarah swear. Come to think about it, neither had he, at least, not in the home and never before women. The pub, well, that was different.

Amid Alice Green's wagging tongue, Sarah heard the violent strapping of his razor on the heavy, leather strap which hung menacingly from the side of the black leaded, kitchen range. Sam's boisterous boys had a healthy respect for that side of the stove. Never a spiteful man, it rarely levered from its bold, brass hook.

The news that Mary Alcock's son was missing brought Sarah sharply into focus as she anguished over Ben, her tall, eldest son. He had answered Lord Kitchener's appeal and taken the King's shilling under a false age and without their permission. Sam had written to the army authorities but so far without success. "Where was he? Silly boy." Her spirits sank further.

Alice, realising that she had made a bloomer, tried to play it down. "Oh, they'd not send a young lad like that to the front

Sarah; it's more than they dare do."

But Sarah was already in the trenches, miles away.

After performing her normal comfort tasks, Alice made her exit with the usual, censuring pronouncement, "If men 'ad the first, the'd never be another."

The children entered the bedroom at Sarah's bidding. For ten days, everything had to be at her bidding. Sam wished the bidding wouldn't arrive with such regularity. It was "do this, don't do that," but he, wisely, never again repeated those offending remarks.

Three year old Jimmy, not yet breached, straddled in long petticoats and grey, smocked frock, climbed the bed to be closer to his mother and eye the intruder who dared take his place. Nesta, eight and Louise, ten, in worn, white pinafores and untidy plaits, lifted five year old Seth for a better look. They squealed with delight. They knew where babies came from, their mother had told them. They came from God, he sent them.

John, twelve, hung back, first on one foot and then the other, his bare legs chapped red by the biting wind. He couldn't be bothered with babies. He wanted to be fourteen and wear longuns; be a man. Why his mother laid in bed was beyond him. But the girls knew, "It's to keep the baby warm."

Nevertheless, they wished she would soon get up. Father, always a laugh, was miserable. The place wasn't the same.

The noisy children, playing outside in the square, suddenly vanished. It must be eight o'clock. Yes, the porter could be heard rounding up the last truants to leave for home or the streets. The four, six storey blocks, so far, the highest in Shadwell, named North, South, East and West faced each other, forming a wonderful playground for the resident's children. Four wooden seats and three high, spreading trees embellished the centre, resting and shading the children by day and gossiping parents on balmy, summer evenings.

The wind dropped. The mocking, full moon sealed its frosty brilliance on buildings and the gently lapping shore. Weary Sam Atkins, his beloved mandolin resting beneath his arm, entered The Bull Pub. Deep in thought, he wavered in the passage before stepping into the smoky clamour of The Sawdust Bar, astir with old and middle aged men, the youngsters away fighting for their country.

The lightermen were being paid out in the bar.

It was a practice that irritated Sarah; viewing it as a diabolical temptation to otherwise good men, the source of Sam's downfall; why he couldn't be moderate like his brothers, Sarah was at a loss to tell.

"Hallo Sam," said Bob Croft, "come to give us a tune?"

"I'll 'ave a pint first," he said sullenly, making his way to the bar stool, and hoping that it would be on the house or slate.

"I 'ear yer've another nipper Sam," said one.

"Yes," volunteered Sam, taking the pint from the blowzy barmaid and supping the froth well in.

"Doing well, ain't yer," chaffed the men. They nudged and winked each other, waiting for his usual retort of "I don't know 'ow it 'appened." But still smarting from Alice Green's revelation, he downed his pint and strummed the mandolin.

Dick Lokes pursed his lips and shook his head before

aiming a bull's eye in the spittoon decorating the hearth and another that missed, hissed the blazing fire. "He knows," he shouted, "he knows."

The company roared with laughter and Sam, ever ready for a joke, joined in the banter. His strumming turned into melodies so delicate and pure, that they ceased shuffling the sawdust and sat quietly, many with closed eyes. He knew how to divert attention.

The plectrum swung with the speed of lightening from one pulsating pitch to another, with the touch and skill of the professional. Music, he had never learnt, but notes etched his brain with a magnetic drive of explosive power.

The noisy jug and bottle crowd, waving jugs of every size and hue, poked inquisitive heads over the separating parapet, and lingered with their wares. They joined The Sawdust Bar. These rough, tough East Enders subdued and enthralled with the wonderful beauty of music from heaven.

The shouts and screams from the street did nothing to break the euphoria, it was nothing new.

The music continued to delight but the shrill whistles of the police forced attention.

"Get those lights out, there's a raid on." The rough voice of authority carried the room.

The silence turned into a crescendo of excited voices and a rush towards the door. Their families were in danger.

The sinister, ominous humming coming from above, grew louder and louder. The men raised troubled brows.

"Look, there she is," went the cry.

From out of nowhere, an oval shaped, balloon like object slid across the sky. Caught in the glare of the full moon, it shone and glittered like spun silver. The dreaded German Zeppelin, its evil intent hidden by its majestic beauty.

Sam, mandolin swinging, raced down the hill and reached the block in seconds. The caretaker had already given the alert and was busy enforcing the blackout. The indoor landings considered the safest, on account of their sheltered position between the flats, were fast filling with panic-stricken families carrying various seats and cushions. Sunken jawed, old men and women, teeth obviously still abiding in salt water on mantelpieces, ambled aimlessly about. Women flopped under long, voluminous nightgowns, their tortuous armour resting on numerous, bed posts. Mrs. McCall was dousing all and sundry with holy water, crossing herself and continuously reciting Hail Mary's. Terror had taken hold. Sam and Sarah nestled their little flock reassuringly against themselves, in crouched positions, the last born snuggled against Sarah's breast.

A strange warmth enveloped her, all else forgotten; the dependent vulnerability of a woman to the strength of a man, her husband.

The advancing hum silenced the fearful, nervous tongues and preceded the terrifying screech of descending bombs. One after another, the devilish screech rent the air. Many of the women, unable to bear the suspense further, screamed with the bombs. The rest sat tight lipped, reconciled to whatever lay before them, for how long they did not remember.

The humming ceased, the danger temporarily over.

Despite the intensity of the raid, only one explosion was heard, the rest fell in the river. God had protected them, the government powerless.

Once over, the inevitable cuppa made the rounds and life returned to normality, until the next king of terrors.

The days passed and Sarah was eager to get up and about, especially to be churched. She was thankful for a safe confinement and a perfect daughter. His hand was upon her and anyway, she knew that unchurched women were forbidden entry into many homes and shops, on the assumption of inviting the devil.

So, early one morning, Sarah slipped quietly out to St. Paul's church. On the way, she passed the fish-market straddled on the shore. Sam had found a job on the trams and she would buy some dabs, at tuppence a pound, on the way home. The children loved the sweet, fresh taste of fish straight from the sea. The fishing smacks from Southend, Leigh-on-Sea, and Chalkwell plied their wares at various places along the river bank. Now she would be able to afford some shrimps and winkles, also a fruit cake instead of the usual seedy cake for the christening. Little Jimmy could be breached at the same time. Her gentle features creased into a smile, amused at the thought of his bare, chubby, little legs pounding the square. Yes, she would kill two birds with one stone, one celebration cheaper than two.

So Sarah knelt at the altar and thanked her Lord for His goodness and a safe confinement, she prayed that this would be her last and that He wouldn't be too cross with her for saying so.

A few weeks later, the christening day set, Sarah draped her baby in the special, lamb's wool shawl kept for the occasion. A broad, tartan sash; a relic from her Scottish ancestry, banded the shawl from top to bottom before curling into a wide bow.

Jimmy, the focus of attention too, skipped and pranced about, eager to show himself off bereft of long petticoats. Louise joyfully carried her little sister, all else forgotten in the excitement of the day and the well being of her mother. The only absentee, Ben, now known to be a private in the cavalry, much to the heartache of the family.

Sam, in collar and tie, full of excuses, arms pinioned back in vice-like grips by Nesta and Ada, brought up the rear. John's high, stiff, white collar dug into his neck. Babies were awful; they brought all kind of traumas. He wasn't having any. So it was, the second tribe of Israel gathered at the font.

The vicar was just about to begin, when the breathless Alice Green, puffing and blowing, made an appearance. From the moment the church door banged behind her, she relayed loudly the reason for the delay.

"Would you believe it, at the last minute, just as I was putting me 'at on, I was called to lay out Joe Scratchit. Stiff as a board 'ee was. Should 'ave called me sooner. It ain't right. What a job I 'ad getting 'is false teeth in, an' 'is eyes closed. An' dirty! Don't reckon 'ees bin washed since 'e be born. 'Ad ter borrer a night-shirt, must 'ave gone ter bed naked, disgusting!" So she went on.

Enough to try the patience of anybody, let alone a vicar, who's authority was never questioned and always had to be addressed as 'Sir'.

    The clergyman was eventually allowed to do his duty and Sarah named her child Cassie. Why, she did not know but Cassie it was. As the water dripped across the little forehead, Sam wondered if he'd have time to get his flagon of beer.

CHAPTER 2

Cassie was an 'it,' only until her first coquettish smile. The wide, blue eyes, outstretched arms and pathetic, little cries impelled and manoeuvred the hardest of hearts, including that of her father's.

"Watcha cock," was his usual mouthy greeting.

She lay, cocooned in layers of greyish, cram flannel, on the shabby, black sofa with the horse-hair poking through. Her eyes shifted from the smoke-grimed ceiling of the kitchen, come living-room, sometimes bedroom, to the popping, broken, gas mantle. It cast its flickering incandescence over flaky walls, hung with tall, fearless clippers battling mountainous seas and the stern, critical faces of the departed. Inquisitive, little fingers explored the bulbed leg of the bare, well scrubbed table centred with the inevitable aspidistra, sunk in a green art pot. The moist, pink tongue bubbled wavering lips. She struggled for the round, drawer knob that held the bane of John's life. His Saturday mornings ruined with brick dust scour on steel blades.

She was everybody's angel, that was, until progression to the crawling and walking stage, then it was a different cup of tea. Nothing was safe or sacred to the marauding, little fingers. Every door, knob, button and handle was pushed, banged or pulled open for further investigation and the contents spewed everywhere. The rustle of torn and crushed paper, usually unread, brought hilarious chuckles of delight. The broad, black beam from tasty, dusty coal sent all except her mother into stitches.

She had also taken to sporting Sarah's old, black hat, topped with a huge, tatty bow and a dangle of grapes, from which she refused to be separated.

Sam's jocular snatches of the hat brought howls of indignation and cries of "me 'at, me 'at."

"She's a caution, she is that, a right case," he would say.

"Yes," commented Sarah with tongue in cheek.

Her patience went for a burton one day at the sight of her flour-bin rolling the floor and Cassie knocking up a pie on the hearthrug, pressing her effort well under the rag-tufts for good measure.

She gave her a resounding whack, that caused the 'at to fall and Cassie to scream long and hard as though being murdered. This brought Lizzie Taylor from upstairs banging on the door, fully expecting to witness a felony. The sight of Sarah, standing with pursed lips and folded arms over the blue in the face, little darling, inflamed Lizzie. She immediately lifted Cassie and gave Sarah a withering look.

"Yer've never laid 'and on 'er, poor little cock," she crooned. "The little angel."

Encouraged by the soft pats, kisses and sh-sh-sh's of her deliverer, Cassie fell into suffocating sobs.

Sarah swore she saw a glint in the tearless, blue eyes as she shouted, "I want me 'at," before being carted off to Lizzie's flat with the promise of a red gob-stopper.

John's comment was, "She 'aves a gate like Blackwell Tunnel."

Sarah vowed there and then, never, never, ever, to lay

hands on the imp again.

Sam roared with laughter.

"Doesn't affect him, so he would," thought Sarah. Nevertheless, she couldn't help feeling that there was something different with this child. "What?" Sarah asked herself. She did not know.

Sarah wearily filled the dented coal-scuttle, from the cupboard next to the kitchen range. It was painted a right 'knock yer eye out' green, as was the larder opposite. She then sank into the rickety, wooden armchair, 'Dad's chair,' at the side of the range. From time to time, she leaned across the bastion of a guard and stirred a bubbling, iron pot, competing with two hissing, black kettles.

Louise and Nesta played cat's cradle, wedged between the sofa and the treadle machine. Cassie, red in the face, was belting the daylights out of the foot of the treadle, the 'at swaying precariously from side to side. Jimmy was under the table, trying unsuccessfully, as he said, "Ter push the 'orse 'air back in the sofa."

Sarah, sick of the noisy, squeaky treadle, threw Cassie a frowsy golliwog. She thought it poor exchange and kicked it away.

"Mum," said Nesta suddenly, "I've got to go to the clinic."
"What for?"
"I've got fleas; I've got to sit at the back until I go."
"Who says so?" said her mother sharply.
"The nurse, Louise as well."

Sarah felt ashamed. It was a losing battle. "I can't understand it," she said, "I'm always at your hair; you must be catching them from the others."

Nesta and Louise shrugged their shoulders and continued with the cat's cradle. Sarah threw off her frustrations in the larder, rummaging for the bits and pieces that transform marrow bones and trotters into a Ritz Special.

"Get me a screw of pepper Nesta," she said, fumbling for the ha'penny beneath the tasselled, mantle drape. She handed the coin to Nesta, "and take this bad egg back." She gave Nesta a cup which she held at arms length.

"Pooh, what a pong!"

"Yer nose too near yer mouth," quipped John, struggling with the complexities of homework. He had been fortunate enough to win a scholarship to the technical school but was, at this moment, wondering upon its merits.

"That's enough," admonished his mother. "And you Louise, fill the pail." The trek to the communal tap and sink at the end of the landing griped Sarah. She yearned for her own kitchen and lavatory too. Mrs. McCall's obsession with the comforts of the seat played havoc with the weekly Syrup of Figs ritual.

Louise opened the door and Mrs. McCall, very distressed and holding her head, nearly fell in.

"Oh me poor 'ead," she moaned.

She was short, fat and smelt of urine. A black shawl covered her bent shoulders and her swollen ankles hung over her slippers.

Sarah drew her in and sat her on one of the six kitchen chairs.

"My, my, Mrs. McCall, whatever is the matter? You look as though you've seen a ghost."

"So I 'ave, Mrs. Atkins, so I 'ave, 'oly Mary," she crossed herself repeatedly and held her head.

"A ghost, never," Sarah smiled.

"I tell 'ee, it were a ghost."

"I'll make you a cup of tea, you'll feel better." Sarah filled the chipped teapot from the impatient, spitting kettle.

"Thank you Mrs. Atkins. I be grateful. May the saints preserve you and yours."

"Did you have a fall?" queried Sarah.

"Far worse, o glory, far worse."

Nesta returned from her errand holding a small paper cone of pepper and an egg. Louise, hanging on every word, still held the pail. Cassie, always eager for fresh excitement, ceased her exertions. The black mole on Mrs. McCall's face and the two long, thick, black hairs sprouting it, took her attention.

"It were to the lavatory I went," continued Mrs. McCall.

"Of course," thought Sarah ruefully, with visions of a locked door and a long wait.

"It's the one place I gets away from 'im." 'Im being her husband. "And ter tell yer the truth, that seat be more comfortable than me own. There I be, all quiet like, praying to the virgin and crossing meself. That chain be 'igh, but I pulled it. It were awful, a legion of devils bashed me 'ead. I'm feared for me life Mrs. Atkins, not bin ter confession fer a week or two." She crossed herself, and Cassie did likewise and kept at it despite a black look from her mother.

"Did you see anything?" asked Sarah sympathetically.

"Nut'ing, nut'ing, them devils, ghosts nearly cracked me 'ead open."

Despite their mother's pokes from behind, the children's shoulders heaved with suppressed laughter.

Sam, home earlier than normal, seemed surprised at the visitor. She was a fairly new tenant, much given to harping on about the evils of the prods. He just saw her as a damned nuisance blocking the bog.

"Allo mate," he said to her breezily, lifting Cassie to the ceiling before noticing Mrs. McCall's distress. "What's up Mrs?"

"She's had a shock Sam, says something awful out there, bashed her on her head. Have a look please." She passed him a lighted candle and Mrs. McCall a cup of tea. Forgetting her head, she graciously took the proffered cup and poured the blessings of every known saint upon their heads.

Sam returned, holding some dirty old bones and a wry look on his face.

"Loads of 'em aht there," he said, eyeing John and the girls with suspicion. They were very silent and subdued.

"It's good to know it's nothing serious," said Sarah, wishing to play it down, but boiling inside. Would they never learn, dirty germ-ridden. God knows they laboured enough with disease, diphtheria, scarlet fever and consumption. Only the other week, Jessie Pike lost her little one with it and five already away with dip'.

Sarah wished she could give the children a copper or two

sometimes. Who could blame them, playing with bones, they had so little.

"I'd like to know who they be, Mrs. Atkins. Them wants a good thrashing. There's one t'ing, I knows it couldn'a be one of your dear ones. They be little angels."

Sarah eager for her to leave, chivvied her to the door. "You'll be alright now dear." The tally-man was due, and she'd pretend to be out. The money all spent on John's school uniform. She'd not have him different.

Hiding her bitterness, Sarah twice tried to help her visitor off the chair but each time she fell breathlessly back. Once Mrs. McCall sat, her legs dropped off. Sam eventually raised the poor, weary, old body. In her haste to outrun the devil, her numerous petticoats and skirt had caught in the waistband. The huge bottom surged the voluminous, smelly, flannel knickers, secured, below the knees with virginal tapes. This set them off giggling again and Sam tried to control his mirth. Cassie's gaze shifted from the mole to the bloated bottom, trying to work out the difference.

Their visitor safely away, the bones down the shoot, the storm broke. The strap nearly off the hook, and the threat of being flayed alive fixed them to the spot. "Nah then, that's the last time I'll talk," he said, "I'll not open me m'ath agin," and smacked his half opened shag on the table.

Taking advantage of the fracas, a determined little fist closed over the shag and equally determined, little legs skived off to the forbidden territory of the lavatory. The candle, left by Sam, shone an eerie light on the black baized, blackout window.

Cassie had been there before but never alone. Her eyes lit up. What wonders of delight. Lovely, newspaper squares dangled enticingly, a seat to be lifted and banged and banged and well, would you believe it, water.

The brown, shag shreds fluttered delicately into the water. The whacking end of the carpet beater, beat her, by its refusal to fit into the pan. Yes, another forbidden item, of course. Temper followed frustration, the neat paper squares, the outward form of high society, followed the shag.

The light finally dawned in Cassie's young head, it was the handle she needed. Frantic agitation produced a miraculous concoction of frothy, slimy, grey pulp, dappled brown. It clung beautifully to the sides of the pan, with the help of a hand of course. Such machinations called for much jumping up and down, banging of the seat and peals of rapturous laughter, tipping the 'at to a precarious level.

A loud, angry voice and hairy arm, brought her raptures to an end.

"Ain't it good eh, look at 'er." Sam deposited Cassie and the carpet beater at Sarah's feet. His indignation knew no bounds. Ter think she could do that ter 'im. The bog of all places, ter put 'is shag dahn the bog.

"Aaht of control, needs ter be taken in 'and."

Cassie sat, the 'at again firmly planted and smiled sweetly. Sarah and Louise had a good laugh. It was another cup of tea when it happened to him.

How the little minx had reached the carpet beater Sarah did not know. Placed high with wistful thoughts of plush tread and polished surrounds. A wonderful setting for the piano that Sam's mother was about to give him. Red and brown would be nice. Brighten up the place a bit. Where the piano was going she hadn't a clue, they couldn't move as it was.

Her musing was suddenly shattered by an almighty explosion that shook the building and sent the family reeling the room. Sam was pinned against the wall. The windows gyrated madly before loudly cracking. The pictures swung from side to side. Aunt Beatie's austere face crashed to the hearth. Cups swung tortuously from their hooks, some smashing. A second explosion followed the first but with less force. The ailing gas-mantle, sizzled, flickered and expired, leaving them almost in total darkness, with just the weak glow of the range.

Sam, dazed, with eardrums bursting, eventually took control and turned off the hissing gas. It was some time before the candlestick was found and lit. The silence was unnerving. "Where or what was it?" There had not been any alert. Anyway, it was too early in the evening for Zepps and they preferred moonlight nights.

The wavering wick sent its pathetic gloom over the stunned family. Cassie clung to her father, who held her tightly. Jimmy's forehead showed red, where he had caught the table. Sarah lifted and hugged him, the others petrified, gathered round, shocked but unharmed. Her eyes spun the room, looking hesitant.

"Seth, Seth, where is Seth?"

Panic took hold.

"Seth!" she screamed, rushing out of the door to the square. "Seth, Seth, where are you?"

He lay, eyes closed, still, white. She lifted him to her breast but he did not move.

"Oh Lord, please not my son! Seth, it's mummy." She shook him, but he was limp.

"Oh Lord, please." She raised her eyes and as she did, saw that the sky to the East was a blood red glow. Great balls of fire shot the sky. It was an inferno.

She screamed, "God help us!" She pressed her little boy closely, seven, just gone. He must have caught the blast. "Not my son Lord, please!" she pleaded.

The sound of running and frightened voices echoed the place but she neither saw nor heard.

She moved automatically and reached the flat. The distressed family gathered round, gently touching their little brother and distraught mother, not knowing how to comfort. Sam tried to be strong but tears filled his eyes. The girls wept softly.

Cassie and Jimmy sensed the anguish, their lips trembling.

A deep sigh broke from Seth's body.

"Mummy, it's mummy Seth," Sarah said quickly. He sighed again and his eyes flickered.

Tears rolled down Sarah's face. God had given him back. "Seth, Seth, it's mummy, everything's alright now." He peered into his mother's face showing no signs of recognition but he was alive.

Sam bent over him, "He'll be fine in the morning gel. It's the blast, in the open that's got 'im."

Sarah placed him in her bed for the night. The next morning, to his parent's delight, he sat up and dressed himself but never said a word all that day, or the next. His mouth moved irrationally but without a sound. Joy turned to despair and bewilderment. The third day he let out a scream and began to cry. He uttered his first word.

"M-m-m-m-m-m-m-u-u-u-m-my," he faltered and struggled. From then on, he was plagued and bedevilled by a stammer, so severe, as to make him almost incoherent. The heartache to his close family was profound but he was alive.

The Sawdust Bar mulled it over and over as to whether the explosion was accidental or sabotage. Buildings and homes nearer to the explosion were wiped off the map and the death toll only surmised.

Everything was hushed up by the government, who perceived information given to the masses as detrimental to the war effort. It cut no ice with the people of Shadwell, or anywhere else. They had long begun to question the folly, producing fatherless children and sorrowing widows, dictated by buffoons in comfortable armchairs, whose only qualifications were those of birth.

As a marine hamlet, death at sea as well as land was never far away. The Atkins and Jamesons had their share of empty chairs and sorrowing widows. Sarah's young brother and Ada's husband were plying the seas. Ben's last letter was six months ago and so censored, as to be almost unintelligible.

Conditioned to either accept or forget the privations of life, Sam and John whistled their way along the highway. They were on their way to collect the joanna. It was many moons since he had sped those ivory keys. Where it was going he neither knew nor cared.

"It could 'elp Seth, Sarah," he cajoled. "I'll teach 'im. I swear I will." He simply bristled with excitement.

They'd bring it 'ome on 'is father's 'orse and cart.

On their way, they passed several hoardings flashing government posters.

"EAT LESS BREAD."

They laughed at the irony of it. "They ain't 'alf sharp."

Often, that's all there was to eat. Another gem:-

"THE GENTLE GERMAN."

It was a picture of a Hun poised with his bayonet and with a baby at the end. It made Sam sick. A more degrading propaganda spectacle he'd never seen. What did they think people were, "tuppence short of a shilling."

Another one, a recruitment poster:-

"JAKE THE SWORD OF JUSTICE."

What justice? He'd never known any. Working twelve hours a day, six days a week, for a pittance. What did they care?

"Can't 'ave a drink with aaht 'em preaching. Taking the food out of the babes m'aths. The hypocritical, smarmy lot, drinks and spends more on booze in a week than a bloke earns in a year. Don't know the thirst of 'ard work."

The arrival of the joanna on old man Atkins 'orse and cart caused quite a stir. The children crowded round Charlie the 'orse, patting and petting him. They gazed with wonder at the posh piano waiting to enter Sam's flat.

Sam and John, proudly wheeled the highly polished, mahogany piano through the square, followed by the usual hoard of kids. The women, gossiping in the square, winked and nudged each other.

"They're coming up."

Others hung from open windows, arms leaning on cream, window sills, commenting upon the quality and gleam of the fashioned, brass candlesticks. No nosy curtain peeps there, insulting the trust of fellow citizens through lack of interest.

Within no time, the block rang out with the old songs he used to play; his whole being rejuvenated. Sarah was happy for him. Her sewing machine banished to one of the three small, overcrowded bedrooms and the coal cupboard partially blocked but she would manage.

Conditioned from birth to either accept or forget sorrow and hardship, the block responded to the music with all their might. They trooped from everywhere, crowded the kitchen and spilled onto the landing, singing their hearts out. Bodies swayed, skirts were lifted and feet tapped the floor.

"Come on Sam," yelled Lil Hankin.

> *"On mother Kelly's Doorstep,*
> *Down Paradise Row,*
> *Sing along Nellie and sing along Joe."*

"Too old for the war, I'll show 'em," muttered Sam.

CHAPTER 3

"I'm owf naah mate," Sam said, not unkindly.

Sarah cringed, as she always did when addressed as mate. She felt like screaming, "I've got a name, I'm a wife, not a mate," but she held back. He had been sober of late; she would not rock the boat.

Sam crossed the square, unaware of the turmoil he had left behind. Even had he known, it would have been dismissed out of hand.

He made his way to the river. The river that had spurned him and taken his mate; the ugly truth forever with him. His mood was heavy. Dense, thick fog hung like a dirty blanket over land and water; making fools of men. Not a light rose from its stifling mantle, the blackout complete.

The blackened, clay pipe bit into his lip, hands thrust the pockets, his steps never faltered. He knew the river like the back of his hand.

Becalmed, eerie skeletons fashioned before his eyes, ghostly shadows churned past, echoing, warning, haunting booms that seared his embittered soul. He was no landlubber. He was no landlubber. Remorse took hold of him. What a fool he had been. His wife, family, they deserved better and Cassie, what secrets stirred in those bewitching, blue eyes?

He toyed with the brass buttons of his khaki greatcoat, pulled tight wrinkled across his broad chest, even that too ill-fitting to be worn with pride. He had enlisted in the fifty sixth London Protection Corp; its local head-quarters, The Sawdust

Bar in The Bull. He slackened his pace and spat into the dark, watery depths. Deep in thought, he lingered off Shadwell pier, his mind in tune with the brooding waters. He wanted to shout, "Go to 'ell, all of yer," but his tongue remained silent, his mood tuned to the river.

Realizing that he would be late for drill, he turned to go but a sound like the soft splash of an oar stayed him. He cupped an ear and could have sworn he heard voices. Who could be about on a night like this? It could be a lighterman making for home. He stood listening but all was silent. His mind was playing tricks, as it often did on such nights. A smile creased his face. Sam's depressions were short lived.

He made to cross the barren fish-market but a murmur of voices, seemingly just below, pulled him up. His body leaned to the water's edge. He gasped and stood rooted to the spot. Deep guttural voices, German, this time there was no mistake. Heart pounding, he scuffed his pipe, lest the pungent odour betrayed his presence. He stood motionless. He was not mistaken. Long association with foreign people familiarized him with all languages and his damaged Seth, resulting from the chemical works explosion, flooded his brain. Heart pounding, he crept, dry mouthed, on tip toe to lessen the crunch of the gravel and made his way to the Highway. They were in peril, the gasworks, ships, all. The Highway reached, he raced to The Bull, and fell breathlessly into The Sawdust Bar.

"Spies," he screamed, "spies."

He was late, and Sergeant Chalky White was mustering his motley squad for drill. They stood at arms, shouldering devastating weapons of war: broom sticks.

"Spies, come aaht quickly!" screamed Sam.

The squad immediately broke rank and crowded around him.

"Shadwell pier," raged Sam. "Get aaht there, call the police."

Buxom Lizzie Turner, the Landlord's wife, began to scream and get hysterical. "We'll all be murdered in our beds, I knew it, I knew it," and ran to the kitchen to get a knife. She returned, screaming and waving a machete.

"Stop it, yer silly cah," yelled her husband Bill.

Chalky White, landed with authority for the first time in his life, was all at sixes and sevens, not quite knowing what to do but thought that he ought to shoulder his rifle; the only one in the squad.

"Come on mates, aaht we go, we'll give 'em what for," he shouted, his knees knocking.

Sam and Chalky led the burnished buttoned twelve; the only shine on the Cinderella army. Fred Lokes's trousers had a row with his boots. Diminutive Eddie Butler appeared to have a hump. Eliza, his wife, never a needlewoman, had cobbled the back with twine, to prevent the jacket sliding from his shoulders. Jimmy Carson's hat hung over his ears. Even the Sergeant's head gear was not in the same place twice. Paddy, Sam's mate, had been issued with one of the old, blue jackets.

They moved silently and quickly, in some semblance of order, down the deserted High Street. The stifling, choking clouds whirled cold and bleak, playing havoc with Nobby

Clarkes chest, causing him to cough and splutter at every turn. Nevertheless, determined to have a go, armed to the teeth with his terrible implement of destruction.

Upon reaching the shingle, leading to the pier, Sam put finger to mouth and bid them stop. Sam and Chalky crept alone, inwardly cursing the fickle shingle. They stood motionless, ears cocked at the pier-head but all was silent, only the soft break of tired water. Long experience told them that the tide was receding. The unmistakable drone of the river police launch broke the silence. Had they been alerted? The comforting drone gradually died away, leaving them with a feeling of isolation. Disappointed, at their lack of prowess, they lingered awhile; bodies poised over the stubborn, locked, murky waters that refused to yield. Sam indicated a quick return to the impatient squad, eagerly waiting to have a smack at the enemy.

The decision to fan out around the fish-market was made. Sam, enviously eyeing Chalky's rifle, kept his company. Eyes smarting, the pair trampled the shore; for how long, they did not know. The fog, if anything, had thickened and the cold and damp bit into them. Chalky's green and red 'kerchief had been left ornamenting the bar stool. His nose was red and sore from constant cuffing of tideless dewdrops on the rough, khaki sleeve.

"Yer sure yer 'eard them voices Sam?" queried the shivering Chalky.

"Of course I 'eard 'em, I ain't daft, them was German as sure as I stand 'ere."

"One voice the same as another ter me in the dark. We're

just looking at nowt. P'raps thems drahned, if it was thems."

"A bone 'ead like Chalky would be at odds to decipher anything, be it in the light or in the dark," thought Sam.

Geared to the unknown, Sam felt deflated. Inwardly, never recognising Chalky's authority, doubts troubled him. What if he had let the men down? Imagined voices, going daft like, leading them on a fool's errand. No, no, he had heard them; spies don't wait to be caught.

As they moved towards Shadwell stairs, Sam clutched Chalky's arm and drew him to a standstill, pointing towards the stairs. Two, barely discernible shapes, hugged the stairway. They seemed to be in difficulty. Their breathing came in heavy laboured gasps. Who were they? Who could they be? Maybe not spies at all. Nevertheless, time was not on their side, they could be armed. It would be foolish to signal for help. They must be taken by surprise.

Chalky, who had never taken anything by surprise, except a pint, stood open-mouthed but thought he must do something, so he cocked his rifle. Sam pulled him unceremoniously to the ground. Afraid even to breathe, they crouched like stalking cats, easing towards their prey. Excitement rising, the fog, a friend for once, encompassed them as they slithered to the top of the stairs, ahead of the intruders. Quick as lightening, Sam sprang and grabbed one man, and Chalky stuck his quivering rifle under the nose of the other.

"Arms up," he quavered, roughly digging the rifle under the armpits.

The two prisoners seemed exhausted and at the end of

their tether. Unable to comply adequately, they made pathetic attempts to raise their arms from their sodden bodies, listing from side to side. Sam quickly frisked them and recovered two revolvers, saturated with mud and grime, possibly useless. Attempts to make them talk failed. Sam blew several times upon his warning whistle. Despite the helplessness of their prisoners, the scurry of running feet was a welcome comfort to their isolation. It seemed so unreal, like a dream.

In no time, they were surrounded with fourteen pairs of gawping eyes. They stood staring at the two sodden, dejected prisoners, definitely in the throes of hypothermia. Two such unlikely spies would be hard to find. Dressed in civilian clothes, they looked little different from their captors. "But why should they?" mused Sam. "Spies don't announce themselves."

It was decided to take them to the pub, before they collapsed. The safety of the people was paramount and dead men tell no tales. A good shot of rum would revive and make them talk.

The two men were assisted to The Sawdust Bar, stinking like sewers and dripping like drowned rats. Chalky, rifle at the ready brought up the rear.

Lizzie's eyes nearly popped out of her head at the helpless, bedraggled pair. From the posters, she expected tin helmet, bayonet, the lot. Her eyes covered the machete.

"Two double rums Lizzie," called Bill.

Lizzie sullenly and slowly poured the rums. "I'd give 'em rum," she said, begrudgingly handing over the glasses.

Bill poured the rum down the throats of the men, their

hands too frozen to hold the glasses.

They perked up a bit, but the rum and heat from the blazing fire appeared to overcome them. They closed their bloodshot eyes and leaned back in the settle. Hatless, their dark hair clung in wet strands about their blue faces and dribbled dirty, brown rivulets down their necks. About a few days growth of bristle hid fair complexions. Their bodies inclined closer towards the welcoming blaze, sending clouds of stinking steam, from their mud soaked clothes, across the bar.

"Pooh, what a ruddy stink," said Sam, aiming a bull's eye into the flame, momentary dampening its goodwill. "They've been in the crap alright."

"Drinks all rahnd," shouted Bill to Lizzie, at the same time, shoving the poker deep into the fierce red glow.

The ale served, he plunged the red hot poker into each pot, activating a sizzling array of sparkling golden bubbles. The men gulped it greedily with much smacking of dry encrusted lips and gobbing squirts in the spittoon.

The bedraggled pair seemed oblivious to all around them, just sitting, huddled together, encased in rising vapour that grew more putrid every second. It spiralled towards Lizzie behind the bar, playing havoc with her curls. They gradually unwound and fell, sorry like, over her podgy, veined cheeks. It was no joke losing your dignity for a whole morning behind an iron foundry, just to end up like a frayed, ragged, wet mop. Her eyes narrowed and her hand went to the machete but not before Bill's hand closed upon hers.

Chalky felt it his duty to interrogate them, to enforce his

role. "What's yer name?" he shouted into the top of their heads, their faces bent, concealed in sodden lapels. "Where yer come from? How long yer bin in England?"

And so it continued, much to the amusement of the bar, his captive audience. They nudged and winked each other, egged him on, encouraging him to think that he had found his lost vocation. Boosted by this unexpected appraisal and much to the dismay of his fellow men, he began to get abusive. Determined to show his authority, he yanked one roughly by the hair and pulled his face towards him. The German, eyes blazing, spat full into his face. He swung backwards, the filthy mess running down his aquiline features. This knocked him and his interrogation for six, sending the 'East End Protection Force' into stitches. Even Lizzie forgot her lost curls and joined in. The prisoner's head simply fell forward to its original pose.

The awaited, army contingent put an end to the hilarity and Chalky's professional stance. The two prisoners were driven away, to where, all were clueless.

Despite the lateness of the hour, the men showed no sign of leaving. The Sawdust Bar buzzed with the events of the night and what might have been, had Sam not been alert. Without doubt, he was the reluctant hero, perhaps saved the whole of London, certainly Shadwell. Embarrassed, Sam wished for his mandolin instead of the broom handle, knowing, as he said, that on all accant, 'e was in the right place at the right time.

Chalky, recovering from shock, tried to get in on it. He sat importantly, his rifle spreading his knee and told how he had cocked his rifle full into the spy's face, nearly blowing his head off. This, he would have done but for the fact of interrogation. He pursed his lips, as he always did, when he thought he'd got one over.

Aubrey Cratchit, always fascinated with guns slid the rifle, unnoticed, from Chalky's knee. Chalky's hands preoccupied with emphasizing his long-winded points.

A puzzled frown crossed Aubrey's face as he pulled the bolt. He paused, then said, "Chalky, it ain't even loaded."

The room went silent. They looked at Aubrey, then at Chalky, before bursting into raucous laughter.

"'Ee deserves a ruddy medal," mocked Nobby Clarke.

Aubrey cocked the rifle at Chalky and said, "A'ms up."

Chalky, the wind knocked from his sails, angrily snatched the rifle from Aubrey. He wished that he had kept his mouth shut but only temporarily. Eager to save his reputation, he retaliated, "It's a clever man who can take a German spy withaaht a shot fired."

"Unless 'e gets yer first," quipped Bill Turner.

But Chalky never heard. His thoughts on the medal that he knew would be awarded.

The good natured banter, ifs and whys, continued into the night, until the first thrust of dawn.

Bill might have called, "Time please," but nobody heard, including the two policemen who, by now, belched noisily.

So it was that the cream of England's army eventually staggered home, well and truly satisfied with themselves.

Chalky's premonition of recognition came earlier than expected. It seemed no sooner had his sleep strengthened to his usual puffing wheeze, when it was broken by police sergeant, Dick Hawkins bashing the knocker. His instructions were that his squad and all who had access to the events of the previous night, were to present themselves within two hours at the local police station.

Sam, like the rest, was snoring his head off. All Sarah's entreaties fell on deaf ears. Cassie, ever willing to help and eager to play, crowned him with the carpet beater; it never seemed in its rightful place. He awoke from his dreams of spies, spies and more spies but not fast enough for Cassie who gave him another crack. He shot out of bed with a start. Cassie laughed and lingered, for, as everybody knew, she could do no wrong.

Outwardly, he cursed the Home Office, police and all. There were boots and buttons to be polished again, yet another shave…. but an order was an order. Barely time to comply, Sarah's queries got nowhere. "Just some fat arsed official," he said. To tell the truth, she couldn't care less. She had Cassie, Jimmy and Seth at home recovering from measles. Jimmy caught it first, so she had bundled Seth and Cassie in with him to save another episode. A darkened room and plenty of sarsaparilla brought them to the present, happy stage. She thanked God that the doctor was not needed, for where would the money have come from?

If there was anybody more in a tizzy than Chalky White, it was Lizzie Turner. All interest in the spies had vanished. She had been 'cawled'. The most important thing on her mind was whether the black suit or the floral one would best suit the occasion. Looking back, and from what she had gleaned from the papers, concerning honours and such like, the dresses and suits were formal or plain. It was hats that took the limelight. Her best black suit would be becoming and firm enough to hold the medal. The hat, with the garland of red roses and cherries cascading the brim, would set it off.

A thrill coursed her frame at the thought of the sword tipping her shoulders. Worried, lest the suit would not allow her to kneel, she donned it and practised in front of the mirror, first on one knee and then the other. She said cheese several times, but decided that a half smile was more fitting for such a serious occasion.

Chalky White, smarting from the night before, wasn't going to get caught out again. He checked three times that his gun was loaded, nearly doing a mischief to Bessie in the bargain. After warning Nobby Clarke to die, rather than cough during the investiture, the whole contingent marched two abreast, broomsticks an' all, to the police station.

The inspector, who always considered himself above such amateur protection, haughtily directed them into a side room.

"Wait here," he said, pointing to some chairs lined up in front of a small table.

The twelve would be soldiers, the two constables, Lizzie and Bill Turner sat stiff and silent, the occasion too important for conversation. Tension rose as the minutes on the bold, round, wall clock ticked away. The half hour signalled a dull thud. It mattered not, for as Lizzie was at pains to voice, "We have been cawled."

The unmistakable grind of brakes told them the call was

nearer.

Repetitive "Sirs, and yes sirs,' rang the corridor, sounding more and more like the crawling Dick Hawkins, thought Sam, this gave way to a tall, khaki clad figure, whose high ranking, smart uniform made a mockery of the East End Protection misfits.

The company immediately stood to attention, saluted, shouldering their fearful weapons. Lizzie, not quite knowing what was expected of her, curtsied before standing to attention, head well raised, following the others.

The Brigadier placed his cane on the table. "Stand at ease," he ordered.

They obeyed, feet apart, Lizzie did likewise.

A bible was sent for and laid on the table.

He spoke in one of those plum, in the gob, uppity voices. "You have been called here at the instigation of the Home Office."

Lizzie's heart thumped and thumped, she knew, she had been 'cawled.'

He continued, "The Home Office wishes to relay thanks for devotion to duty."

"Danger too," thought Chalky.

"You are also here to take an oath of secrecy concerning the events of last night."

He stopped and gazed along the line. "The Home Office has the last say and judgement on these matters. Any deviations will be recognised as treason and punished accordingly."

Lizzie trembled, her 'cawling' left dangling at the end of the hangman's rope. Her legs gave way and fourteen stone fell gasping to the floor.

The Brigadier never turned a hair. "Pick that woman up," he said in a matter of fact tone.

The stunned 'cawled', could hardly believe their ears. Bill and Sam assisted the sweating Lizzie to a chair. Her best stockings holed, her hat rolling the floor when her curls, unfortunately, began to enter the race.

Here they were, after risking life and limb, now subject to treason.

"You will come," he said as though talking to the furniture and place your hand on the bible and swear an oath to God, King and Country, never to reveal anything of what transpired last night to any living person, or persons, either now or hereafter."

As though in a trance, one at a time, they took the oath of secrecy. Their lips sealed for all time.

The greatest adventure of their lives swept under the carpet but it did not still the tongues of the sixteen amongst themselves. A German submarine had managed to reach Tilbury at high tide; this, as gospel from the lightermen. Could this explain the embarrassment of the government, caught with their trousers down, the devastation at the chemical works and many other unexplained incidents?

Lizzie's ego smashed, she could never look at the hat with the roses and cherries, or the black suit, without feeling humiliated and let down. It cut her to the quick to be denied centre stage in the gossip stakes, also not to have one over that stuck up Nancy Tricker. Her oath was sealed more through fear than loyalty; even the hawser rope sweated her brow and made her feel faint.

Fred Lokes, one of the number, kept quiet concerning his early morning meeting with Gussie Kcy'ole, as they walked their dogs, after all, it was before the oath.

Gussie, never large in the community and the biggest blabbermouth this side of the Thames, suddenly outshone Lizzie in the gossip stakes. He embroidered every word ever uttered from Fred's mouth and gullibly laced the edges.

The tale went that the East Enders had fought hand to hand with a legion of German spies on Shadwell pier. Also, that Lizzie had chopped one in half with a machete.

Lizzie, deprived of what she considered her rights, neither denied nor admitted the story. She upheld the oath with a cunning smile and shrug of her hearty shoulders, considering it her perks for the humiliation and shock that she had suffered, plus the medal denied her.

The contingent, having recovered from the initial disappointment, treated it as just another one of their experiences and contributions to the war effort. Never again would dock patrol be treated as just another chore, especially as the broomsticks gave way to rifles.

Sarah listened to the gossip with a pinch of salt. She had other things on her mind. Cassie, after much delay, through illness, was ready for nursery school.

CHAPTER 4

Cassie sat solemnly upon the stool, whilst her mother bedded her tiny feet in the newly repaired boots. She had been spectator to her father's cobbling, in the hope of knocking in a few herself and had watched with beady eyes where he had homed his tools. Her eyes followed the round up of six, reluctant, black-knobbed buttons by the determined steel hook. She thought hard. "Would school be on a par with home and Auntie Taylor's gobstoppers?" She fiddled with the white bow that gathered the ginger hair from off the freckled forehead and ran her fingers along the nappy pin, that seared the breast of her stiff white pinny and held the length of rag; the regulator for long, runaway candles.

With an air of abandonment, Sarah straightened herself from her labours. "There you are dear," she said happily, "all ready."

Sarah's hand tightened on Cassie's but she refused to budge. Looking straight into her mother's eyes, she blurted out,

"I ain't going."

Sarah thought it wiser to ignore the ain't. "It'll be lovely Cassie. Miss Noble lets you make sandcastles and mud pies."

"Jimmy said, Miss Noble, old fat guts."

Sarah's abandoned air gave way to irritation. "Jimmy's a naughty, naughty boy."

"I *ain't* going," said Cassie, deliberately emphasising the ain't, and determined to have one over her mother.

"The Queen went to school Cassie," said the deflated Sarah, calling upon Cassie's love of dressing up as the Queen.

Cassie beamed, jumped up and pointed to the hat dangling from the door. "Me 'at, me 'at, I want me 'at," she cried. "I want to be Queen."

"Have it when you come home dear," cajoled Sarah. Miss Noble was a stickler for convention.

"Me 'at, me 'at, I want me 'at," she screamed.

Sarah's patience wore thin. She grabbed the hat from the hook and smacked it upon the errant head. Anything for a quiet life, "Who cares? Let clever click Miss Noble have it."

Cassie held her mother's hand; her eyes squinted mischievously from beneath the hanging grapes. They passed the biscuit factory, and sniffed its appetising aroma. The normal parade of gaily decorated carts and slender, chestnut horses now reduced to a few dowdy carts and weary nags, the rest sent to die, with their riders, in Flanders graveyard.

The noisy, clacking tin factory spilled its waste of sharp, tin cuts across pavements and streets. Three, bare-footed urchins cautiously picked their way through the hazardous litter, pausing to playfully tilt Cassie's hat. She responded with her infectious laughter and they, with broad smiles and cheeky winks.

Downside of the Radcliffe Highway, the once bustling Fish Market lay. The grey waters lapped and mocked the voiceless, barren shingle, where, earlier, the calls of bearded fishermen and jesting, jostling housewives rang.

"Shrimps, cockles, whelks, the best in the country. Fish straight from the sea. It's all 'ere."

The sun mocked and beamed its scintillating rays of spangled gold over each bounding wave. Sarah's thoughts turned to her family. Ada's husband, Joe, at sea, and Ben, in France, caught up in the madness. Turning to go, she stopped. A limping, holed sloop came into view. It cowered, deep below the waterline, desperately struggling for home. Its shrill, pain stricken cry rent the air. Sarah held her breath. How long could it hold? The deep sonorous boom of approaching tugs gave succour to the stricken vessel and Sarah heaved a sigh of relief. They came swiftly portside of the vessel. Only when she saw the heave of the ropes did she feel ready to leave. A sense of pride stirred her. Sam had been reinstated. He would be among the rescuers.

The school, a large, grey, forbidding building was situated further up the Highway, opposite the docks. Its narrow windows perched high to avoid distraction of any kind. Apart from the infants, separation of the sexes was on a par with a monastic order.

Sarah trod warily upon entering the school grounds, and Cassie's grip tightened. They were late. They entered the classroom or 'babies' as it was known and stood just inside the door. It was surprisingly quiet. About thirty little children sat with folded arms, on infant chairs, facing Miss Noble's desk. She was round in every quarter, except her nose which was long and thin. Her mousy hair formed a hard ball at the back of her head. She eyed Cassie and Sarah above steel-rimmed spectacles.

"Mrs. Atkins, I take it?" she said abruptly. "You are late."

Sarah moved towards the table. "Yes," she said meekly,

"I am sorry."

"And I suppose," continued Miss Noble, "this is Cassie Atkins."

"Yes," said Sarah "and this is Cassie's lunch." Sarah handed over a white, paper bag, twisted at the corners, containing two slices of bread and dripping.

Miss Noble wrote Atkins upon it and threw it into a basket. "I should take that monstrosity with you," she said, pointing to Cassie's hat.

Sarah made to lift it, but Cassie, grim faced, held on with both hands, Sarah, knowing the blast of her lungs was reluctant to go further.

"It was the only way I could get her here," said Sarah apologetically, trying for another go, but Cassie, white knuckled, held fast. Sarah drew back. Miss Noble eyed her contemptuously and grabbed the crown with a fat hand, leaving Cassie, empty handed and screaming at the top of her voice.

Sarah slunk out, abandoning the distraught child to the doubtful attention of Miss Noble. She felt no guilt, only elation. For the first time in twenty four years, she was free, and laid the red carpet, leaving Miss Noble, without doubt, to roll up hers.

Cassie never did like Miss Noble, and thought many times about running home but knew, too well, her mother's reaction, besides which, she had a fearful dread of Miss Noble's hard slap.

The aggrieved child regularly relayed to her family the

intrusion of Miss Noble in her life.

"The rocking 'orse isn't bad but it's not like our sofa, with Jimmy as driver. Yer mustn't shout loud 'gee ups.' It couldn't be a boat either. Yer 'ad ter sit on chairs and not talk." She gave a twisted smile.

"She'd give yer a smack if yer talked. Yer couldn't dress up." Cassie gave the straddled straw of the long suffering hat a couple of twists.

"Playtime's funny. We all line up in front of Miss Noble with our clothes up. She undoes the buttons of our drawers. We then run to the lavatory in the playground with our clothes up. I told 'er, it were rude to show your bottom."

"An' what did she say?" smiled Sam.

"She pushed me, and said, 'get on.' She's not very good doing buttons up. I told 'er, our mum's got an 'ook, but she didn't answer. She smacked Tommy Falls for weeing himself. It was all on the floor. We 'ave ter go to sleep in the afternoon. The big girls, from upstairs, turn our tables upside down and tie a sheet to them. I close my eyes and pretend, or she gives yer a slap. Miss Noble's lazy. She reads a book. P'raps John'll take me down to the shore. I found some lovely stones there yesterday. I don't like Miss Noble."

So it was that the amused family received Cassie's version of early school days. Sam picked her up and threw her over his shoulder.

"Yer did well cock," he said proudly, "yer did well."

Cassie was unwell. She lay pale and listless upon the sofa. Sarah had tried to ease the sore throat with honey and lemon, but became alarmed when her eyes glazed and she seemed unaware of her surroundings. Alice Green, the connoisseur on babies and throats was sent for.

She waddled, puffing and blowing, through the door, full of complaints. "Rushed owf me feet gel, overdue is Pearl, I've dosed 'er with caster oil but stubborn that's what it is, a boy fer sure. Thems starts owf awkward and ends awkward." She plonked herself next to the child, and patted her head. "There, there, we'll soon see what this is about luvvy."

She took the proffered spoon from Sarah and pressed the child's tongue down with the handle, and gasped. "Oh my Gawd!"

"What is it Alice?" said Sarah abruptly.

"She's got it." Alice Green's eyes met Sarah's.

"Got what, got what?"

Like all carriers of bad news, the words dragged slowly. "The dip, the dip Sarah!"

Sarah froze, her face blanched.

"It doesn't always go 'ard Sarah, Cassie's strong." Feeling that she had to give a sense of direction to the shocked mother, added, "Get the doctor. Dr. Lynch, 'e's the cheapest."

Annie Taylor, who had seen and heard Alice Green's entry, eagerly offered to fetch the doctor for her little darling. "Poor little cock," she fussed, "poor little cock."

The portly Dr. Lynch, who hadn't seen his feet for years, stepped heavily from his cab, leaving the driver aloft the pawing hack. Bag in hand, he ponderously crossed the square, cheeks ballooned with the exertions of his pace. Irish, blue eyes twinkled beneath a jaunty, black topper. The buttons on the wrinkled, shiny, black jacket promised to pop at any moment in their struggle to keep uniform his expanding girth. He strode knowingly to the door, knocked and entered.

Sarah quickly offered him a chair beside the sofa into which he fell, breathing heavily.

"She's fair poorly doctor, it's her throat."

"A spoon my dear," he requested kindly.

Cassie obediently opened her mouth, whilst he, with the aid of a tiny torch scrutinised her throat. He paused, as though reluctant to speak.

"I am afraid Mrs. Atkins," he said slowly, "it is diphtheria. She will of course have to go to isolation."

Sarah swayed, and he gripped her hand sympathetically. All hopes that Alice Green's diagnosis could be wrong, dispelled.

"The little lass'll get well, be home in no time." He patted her shoulder soothingly.

Sarah took one shilling and sixpence from her purse, but he pushed it aside.

"Nay, nay, all 'll be well, you'll see, nay, not to worry too much." With one last comforting pat he left the room.

Sarah was heartbroken but knew not to give way. This was the first time the dip had knocked upon her door.

Now alone, she was filled with remorse. The guilt of the unwanted birth. Her impatience and indifference to the screaming child's first day at school, crowded her mind. The sight of Cassie's pathetic remnant of a hat, dangling from the door, sent her into floods of tears. diphtheria, the killer. The thought of her child, alone, perhaps dying, tore her to pieces. She felt unable to pray, her body bent double, tears soaked her pinny. God's punishment was upon her.

Within a week, Jimmy, Seth, and Louise entered the isolation hospital and Sarah felt akin to Christ on the Cross, "Oh God, why has thou forsaken me?"

Sam's support was nil. He did what she'd known he'd do, drown his sorrows in the wretched Sawdust Bar and deprive her of money. Louise's letter that Cassie's face was a mass of sores, coupled with the fact that visits were taboo, sent him into a vile temper.

"Even if it was allowed," placated Nesta, "it's right off the beaten track dad, you'd never get there."

"I'll show 'em, the cheeky gits," he stormed. "I'll get the 'orse and cart aaht, I'll show 'em. On all accahnt, they can't refuse yer and they ain't gonna."

Evidently, The Sawdust Bar had been a hive of information.

"Yer thinks thems with lolly don't see their kids? It's them that brings the fevers, farting 'alfway rahnd the world to fry their fat arses in the sun."

Grandad Atkins wasn't at all taken up with the idea of using Charlie the 'orse.

"Ee ain't a youngster yer know Sam, Gawd knows what 'ee'd catch there."

"Don't be daft dad, 'orses ain't 'uman, they don't 'ave it," said Sam, dismissive of any argument.

"I ain't so sure abaht that," Grandad continued, "Aubrey Bright's 'orse 'ad fever."

Eventually, with Grandad Atkins won over, Charlie washed down with the Jeyes Fluid, harness burnished as never before, they jangled their way through Wanstead to the edge of Epping Forest. It certainly was off the beaten track. Sarah revelled in the green surroundings and Charlie seemed to enjoy his excursion. He trotted up the tree-lined drive as though he owned it and came to a halt outside a large, imposing, Manor House. A heavy, oak panelled door barred the entrance, almost shouting "Don't you dare!" They sat staring, evaluating the position. Grandad's eyes flickered back and forth, from Charlie to the door. Sam's eyes narrowed and Sarah trembled.

"Well it ain't gitting nowhere sitting 'ere is it?" said Sam. Descending the cart he stamped up each of five stone steps to the door.

"Come on you two," he reprimanded.

Sarah moved slowly and Grandad followed but not before he emptied the rest of the Jeyes Fluid on Charlie's rump. "Yer never knows," he muttered.

Sam, without hesitation, pulled the cord of the ancient, brass bell. They heard its toneless, summoning clang reverberate through the forbidding building. They waited and Sam impatiently gave a second pull.

The creaking door partially opened and a head protruded from it.

"Well?" she said, bringing herself a little more into view.

Sarah could see that she wore the uniform of a maid.

Sam spoke, "We're Mr. and Mrs. Atkins, we've come to see aah kids missis."

Her eyebrows lifted in surprise. "I'll bring Sister," she said, banging the door shut.

"That's nice, ain't it? About as welcome as a pork pie in a synagogue," Sam said irritably.

A tall, slim, white frilled, capped woman came to the door. "I am afraid visitors are not allowed," she said haughtily.

Sarah blanched. The woman continued, "If you want to know how they are doing, they are doing very well Mr. Atkins."

"We ain't come all this way Missis with the 'orse and cart and not see aah kids," Sam retorted angrily.

"It's against the rules Mr. Atkins," she said, making to shut the door, but Sam already visualised her intent and pushed past her.

"Git aaht me way woman, where's me kids?"

Clearly startled, she held her ground, "How dare you!"

Ignoring her, he cocked his thumb to Sarah and father, "Come on." Old man Atkins gave one last look at Charlie and followed with Sarah into the vestibule.

The Sister pressed a handbell on the table and almost immediately a white coated man made his appearance, obviously, having been informed of the awkward trio.

"I understand that you wish to see your children." He spoke courteously.

"That's aah motive mate," said Sam.

"This is an isolation hospital Mr. Atkins, it is simply not

allowed."

"On all accant, yer can't stop us. I knows me rights, so yer best let us in to 'em. We ain't come all this way with the 'orse and cart mister fer nothing." Sam made to move into the adjoining corridor but the white-coated doctor moved swiftly ahead.

"Wait," he said, with a shrug of his shoulders, "I will take you."

He led them to a small annexe and from one of the many cupboards he pulled three smocks. "Put these on please," he said politely.

Completely enveloped in the long shroud like gowns, they followed the doctor along endless corridors that reeked of disinfectant. He stopped in front of a wide, glass window, from where could be seen Cassie and Jimmy in bed, side by side. Louise was up and amusing them. They were obviously recovering well but Cassie's face, as Louise wrote was a mass of sores.

"It would be better if you did not go in," entreated the doctor but Sam was already at the door. The children did not at first recognise their father in his unusual get up. Soon cries of "Dad, dad," rent the air. They were beside themselves with joy.

Sarah emptied her little bag of goodies; chocolates, oranges and books. Louise gave a graphic account of the loving care given by the overworked nurses, which gave Sam a temporary sense of guilt, for his former rough speaking. Sarah sensed the mystery of God's ways that enabled her babies to have a second mother in Louise. She prayed fervently that God would forgive her lack of trust.

The little ones clung tearful at their departure. Louise comforted them with the knowledge that they would soon be home.

Sarah, eager to make amends for their forced entry, thanked the Sister profusely, spoilt of course by Sam.

"It's aah right," he bawled, "they ain't give us nothing."

The journey home was a happy one. Sarah had never seen Sam so elated, neither had The Sawdust Bar, who reminisced long afterwards, how, "On all accant, that plum gobbed lot got a smack in the eye."

The children's return home called for a celebration. A fruit cake centred the table and the muffin man, whose voice was on a par with the 'town crier,' waylaid. He served the family from the precariously balanced tray, with a big smile and two extra for luck, then, with a powerful swing of his brass hand bell, went on his way.

Cassie's school days were mostly one of battle and hate. The teachers all used the same red tipped, white rod to knock in what you ought and knock out what you ought not.

With her eye on the first chance to earn a copper, Cassie once asked if they had any babies. They turned a terrible, meat colour and gave an emphatic, shocked, "Certainly not!"

Cassie thought that if she had posh clothes instead of hand-me-downs, she'd stand more chance of being a monitor and be called Cassie instead of Atkins, like Phylis Carter the policeman's daughter or Rhoda the fireman's.

Enthused with her new slate and artistic ability, Miss

Noble, Miss Gates and Miss Keyole ran the gauntlet of Cassie's wrath and indignation, with long warty noses, gaping mouths, crossed eyes, rabbits teeth and shocks of hair permanently in fright. This gave the class hysterics and Cassie the red tipped rod. Her encounter with the long, thin cane came later, during one needlework lesson.

Phylis Carter and Cassie were tasked with a long run and fell on an unmentionable. Miss Keyole smiled and hovered over Phylis Carter.

"Beautifully executed Phylis, very neat," she burbled, despite her stitching dog's teeth, whilst Cassie's was passed over. It was the way Phylis Carter leaned across and smirked. Straight in went that needle, straight in to that nosy nose. A murder victim couldn't have made more fuss. It drew blood and gave great satisfaction. It was to that meddlesome, doughty woman that the armed assailant was sent. She, who insisted on red ribbon if you wore white, her sadistic nature appeased with three of the best.

But it was a Miss Bastow, on the way up to the seniors, who recognised Cassie's ability and made her monitor, despite her jumble attire. Unfortunately, it backfired.

It was Friday, and the monitors were instructed to purchase an afternoon treat from the biscuit factory.

"Get your coat dear," Miss Bastow said kindly.

That coat was the last thing on earth ever to parade around in. A relic of the past, if ever there was one, at least one hundred years old. There Cassie stood, facing the class in the long, grey, woollen coat, that boasted, three heavily embroidered capes and frilled embroidered cuffs. The last bones of the boot box encased her feet, boy's boots. Sly giggles ran through the class and Cassie vowed to burn the Methodist Church and their jumbles, along with their itchy combinations, also, the know-all who made her wear glasses. Sadly, she reflected that with ginger hair and four eyes, she was no oil painting.

Returning home, the strong smell of Sloan's Liniment greeted her. Sloan's was usually kept at Grandad's to be used upon the horse. Mother was diligently rubbing father's poorly back. He sat in his armchair waiting for a miracle. The family watched, open mouthed, his fair skin turn a fiery crimson, along with his temper. His face screwed with pain, he snatched the offending bottle from Sarah, and read:

"On no accahnt rub, pat gently."

He threw the bottle to the floor. "You silly bitch," he screamed, can't yer read? I ain't no 'orse!"

Unable either to sit or stand, he strode the room, shouting things normally reserved for the pub.

Cassie sat petrified, in silence, whilst the rest of the family held their breath. Sarah, nearly in tears, frantically daubed his scalding back with cold water. Gradually, it dulled to a salmon pink and he fell exhausted in his chair, still mouthing threats.

All present heaved a sigh of relief but not for long. He began to pull strange faces as though in a stroke or fit. Close inspection revealed that the arm of his spectacles had caught between his teeth and refused to budge; a habit he had when vexed, of sliding the arm up and down his teeth.

Not knowing whether to laugh or cry, they watched the

appendage sway from his gaping mouth. A sudden tug severed not only the arm but the tooth as well, leaving him bawling, shouting and dripping blood. Eventually, to the family's relief, he left to be cleansed in The Sawdust Bar.

Following a calming down period, Cassie and Jimmy renewed their game. Jimmy drove two horses like mad; bringing his whip down and clicking his tongue just like Grandad. Robbers were chasing them. It was so exciting. Cassie was eager to be the driver for once. Jimmy kept on that girls can't be drivers. It didn't matter how much she told him they could. Then, he said that Jesus had told him that he'd got to be the driver. Cassie hadn't heard Jesus say anything; she clouted him hard with the carpet beater, the one she'd used to fend off the robbers. He screamed blue murder, baby that he was.

Sarah, already riled with dad and Seth; Seth had been playing Germans and got his head stuck in the po, plastered them all with a wet towel from the fire guard. She'd never been a one, thought Cassie bitterly, to find out whose fault it was first. The only thing to be done was to make a run for it and think of better times, like market day.

Cassie loved market day, so next morning, she was up like a lark and off with her mother, large bag in tow. There, she eyed the stalls piled high with colourful fruits and vegetables.

"Sixpence a pahnd apples and pears, come on gels, yer do no better, spuds two pahnd for thre'pence."

The cries of the barrow boys rose above the disorder of gossiping women, raucous laughter, screaming children, tramping feet and barking dogs. Stalless, Joe, scattered the pavement with his jumble of outdated, second-hand clothes. Known in jest as "Longehayes on the ground," reminiscent of the posh shop Longehayes, in the main road, where Sarah and her kind just looked and wished. He brought his own peculiar patter, the coarse Music Hall prattle. A tatty boa straddled his scrawny neck, and sly, titillating flips accompanied each suggestive innuendo, spurring the less sensitive into crude response. Only the brave or desperate bought unmentionables.

They meandered left and right between boys scrambling beneath stalls for left-overs, heavy crates and muscled men, whose mouths like their arms never tired. The unsmiling woman who painfully grated large tubers of horseradish, whilst loudly reminding women of their duty.

"Don't let the old man go wiv aht, give it 'im 'ot." The neighbouring vendors noisily added their own humorous innuendoes, and Sarah pulled Cassie away.

The occasional drunk staggered the street under the watchful eye of the policeman. White, aproned Jack Soloman, slated his slow paced assistant, as his fish peered mournfully from beneath the arms of Polish, Jewish immigrants, whose momentary vision was one of boiling oil and fennel.

The hardware shop was a maze of socks, barrels, boxes and cases filled to overflowing with soap powders, soap flakes, soda, hearthstone, brick dust, candles and other queer things, which left little room for feet. Most things were sold 1d per handful, including the soft soap that plastered the kids hair every Saturday. A bar of lifebuoy soap and a handful of Hudson's completed the purchase. They were given a send off, as though millionaires, by the warm Jewish shopkeeper.

Except for its more appetizing smells of spices and dried fruit, the grocers was little different from the shambles of the hardware shop. Cassie watched the struggling victims on the sticky brown fly papers that hung innocently from the ceiling and gas mantles. Sarah bought two for threehapence. Cassie picked her way inquisitively round the shop before being hailed by her mother on her way to the butchers. It irritated Cassie the way her mother gawped, hand on mouth at the butchers. Dad said, "Yer mum counts the pimples on the belly of pork," though she'd never noticed them until he said. The only thing to do was to make patterns in the sawdust.

She had seen her mother pop a bag of locust beans in the sack bag with the tart remark, "Wait until you get home."

The long brown shrivelled bean belied its succulent sweet flavour and Cassie couldn't wait to get home.

A man sold birds and people took them home in a paper bag. A man, without legs, sat on the pavement. Mum put a halfpenny in his cap. She said, "The war did it."

Cassie was fascinated by words, especially adverts. Ex Lax, Unoes Fruit Salts, Sloan's Liniment, never to be forgotten, and Bile Beans for flatulence.

"What's flatulence dad?" she queried. It was no good asking mum on Saturday's, she never seemed to hear you, or didn't want to.

He paused, and then said loudly, "Wind."

Sarah gave him a black look, screwed her mouth and

turned her nose up. Bile Beans had never been his saving grace, nor any at The Sawdust Bar.

Chewing locust beans, Cassie followed Seth, John and their mates to the shore. She knew her place. It was to be coppers nark, whilst they plundered the banana barges.

It was low tide and the barges lay sleepily just beyond the shore. Cassie sat on the warm, shingled shore surrounded by small piles of clothes. A quick retreat was always on the cards. Their mentor, in the form of Flat Footed Jack was never far away. She eyed the bundles of patched and torn trousers, also the holed socks of her brother's mates, though 'arry Beanstrope, had one up, by never wearing any. Mum never allowed pins or 'oles, only itchy combinations.

She watched their flaying, naked bodies close in towards the barges. Playfully, Cassie threw stones in the water and marvelled at the widening circles, from which flashed the elongated body of an eel braving the dirty waters. How peaceful, the river, she loved it and couldn't imagine life without it.

Into her thoughts came the purpose of her vigil and she turned her head to the Highway. A group of noisy, laughing boys emerged from a building and from behind a black figure. Was it or wasn't it? It grew larger and rounder. Yes it was him! She could see the swinging, black cape. It was Flat Footed Jack. To be taken home by him was worse than death. Unclasping her knees, she stood and frantically waved one of the grey vests as she'd never waved before. Almost immediately, the water became a fretted mass of white foam. Cassie had forgiven Jimmy and held his trousers at the ready. They reached the waters edge, dripping, breathless and slimy; Seth still bore the angry hallmark of the po. All the time the portly policeman was closing fast. Water, never a handicap before, bedevilled them, tying shirts and vests into knots. On and on he came. A searing rip and Seth's bottom showed pink above the jagged patch, but tremulous thoughts were banished in the fear of the moment. Wet, grubby hands seized hers and with flying bootlaces and angry shouts from behind, they went like the clappers, Cassie's feet never touching the ground until the safety and warmth of the Gas Works was reached.

"You so and so's, here again?" roared the coke man.

It was bath night. Sarah half filled the zinc bath with water from the bucket and boiling water from the stove. It was a small bath, Cassie sat with bended knees, whilst her mother soaped her with the pink lifebuoy soap and shampooed her hair with the gooey, soft soap. Louise dried her and Sarah added more water, with the anecdote, "Dirty water washes clean."

Jimmy stepped in. He smelt rotten, causing mother's nose to twitch. The twitch was followed by a resounding whack upon his bottom which resulted in a scream.

"You've been in that river again, haven't you?" she yelled, bringing her hand down again, leaving Jimmy sobbing violently and Cassie and Louise trembling. She could really get going when she started.

"I suppose you've been there too?" she shouted, directing her attention towards Seth. Seth, who wished that he could go to the public baths like John, was hurriedly undressing lest the waving patch caught his mother's eye; but it was too late. She tore the trousers from him and laid into him like a mad woman.

Louise burst into tears. "Mum, stop, mum, you'll kill him," she cried, positioning herself between her mother and Seth.

Sarah, aghast at what she was doing, pulled back, leaving all the children frightened and sobbing. What was she thinking of? What kind of mother was she?

Louise knew that they would be having sausages for Sunday dinner tomorrow. Sam, with more money in his pocket, not only was drinking but gambling. Sarah put her arms round her little boy and cuddled him. "Mummy does love you," she said, and handing him over to Louise she vanished, weeping, into the bedroom.

It was early to bed. Cassie lay with the subdued Jimmy at the foot of the double bed, and pondered the events of the day. She missed her father. He hadn't been around for six days, leaving early and returning late. She cast the heavy, old coat that stood in for a blanket to one side, and pulled up the well patched sheet. It was hot and the window had caught on the broken sash, limiting the flow of air. The railway arches opposite, housed the unfortunate horses in the fly-ridden stables and the trains belched their doubtful welcome of black, acrid smoke. It all seemed in keeping with her mother, who was nearly always sad.

It was Sunday tomorrow and Cassie would wear her best

dress and go with her brothers and sisters to Sunday school. They would sing 'Jesus Bids us Shine,' and 'Wide, Wide as the Ocean.' She loved it. Jimmy and Seth loved it so much that they got thrown out, though she never let on.

She dwelt on the possibility of accompanying her father to Sophie Fisher's christening celebration, knowing also, that her mother wasn't keen. She could tell by her nightly prayers that her mother was troubled and that it was something to do with the horses and The Sawdust Bar. In the still of each late evening, her voice would rise higher and higher. Full of reproaches against herself, "Forgive me Lord for my many shortcomings. Give me patience. Keep your hand upon my children. Keep Sam on the straight and narrow Lord. Keep him away from the horses."

Cassie wasn't quite sure what the last meant. Mother was very holy. She went to the Methodist Mother's meeting and jumble sale on Tuesdays, the Salvation Army and jumble on Wednesdays, the Quakers on Fridays and sometimes church on Sundays; but not very often. She somehow thought that if dad was holy, her mother wouldn't get into such a do.

The following Saturday, dressed in her Sunday best, she took her father's hand and traversed the streets to Sophie Fisher's, sixth christening celebration; despite her mother's disapproval.

A nifty red and green necktie adorned Sam's neck, whilst his mandolin caressed his left arm. They passed the docks to the bonded warehouses, gorged with romantic, eastern spices.

The strong, sweet, pungent aroma pervaded every nostril and every home thereabout, without even a thought. The tall, dreary, iron-barred warehouses, broken only by 'The Cocked Eye' pub, dwarfed the little terraced houses opposite.

They stopped at number ten, Sam lifted the latch and calling "Sophie," entered, then gave his feet a good scrubbing on the coconut matting; Sophie was very particular. Her front parlour opened only on Christmas days or for christenings, funerals and the vicar. She kept the key in her pocket.

She was a tall, generously built, handsome woman of about thirty six. She greeted them warmly, Cassie, as usual, introduced as the youngest.

The ten foot, square parlour smelt of stale air and wax polish. The oiled aspidistra centred the brown chenille, draped table. Pictures of the living and the departed, graced every conceivable space, except one on the whitewashed walls. The blank held a pink and blue ribboned grotto, adorned with stiff white bows. The uninviting, stiff-backed chairs boasted lace antimacassars but it was the beautifully embroidered fire screen that took Cassie's eye. It stood teasingly pompous alongside its stale companions, overriding even the scratched piano.

"Aah's Sarah?" enquired Sophie.

"Same as usual," said Sam indifferently, placing his mandolin alongside his brother's less conventional instruments.

"Aht 'ere," he beckoned Cassie, pointing towards the noisy hubbub of the living room.

All living rooms were much the same, kitchen stoves, rag rugs, scrubbed tables, hard chairs and pictures. A defused, six inch, brown hand grenade sat central on the mantelpiece, adjacent to a glass tumbler which usually held Grandad Fisher's, grinning choppers. A huge barrel of beer wobbled precariously upon a creaking fruit crate. Sophie's husband Jack, a tall, angular docker, took control of the ever running tap and his beer swilling mates.

In the wash house the women busied themselves with the needs of the stomach and followed with cynical contempt the hurried comings and goings of leaky, male bladders to the back yard.

"On all accant," said Sam, with a final touch of his fly. "All new 'ahses are 'aving the bog inside."

The women turned their noses up.

"Not in my 'ahse they wouldn't, pooh!" said Eliza Penfold, "filthy!"

The women nodded in affirmation, with cries of "No fear," and Sam made a hasty retreat. Eliza Penfold turned her mind to other matters. "Of course, it's said, that Fred Lokes son-in-law is carrying on with Nancy Jardine," she whispered, "but keep it under yer 'at."

"Of course Eliza, of course." The women went into a huddle.

"'Im with four kids, ought ter be ashamed of 'imself," said Mary Arkright. "God 'elp 'im if Fred finds 'aht."

Cassie joined the excited children playing in the yard but the sound of the piano belting out McNamara's Band sent them flying into the house. With the addition of mandolin, clappers and drums, the music got bold and fast. Jack's father, old Tom

Fisher, took centre stage. His short rickety legs, never obstacles, sent them reeling with laughter. Jack, donned Sophie's hat and engaged in mimicry play. This sent Tom into further gymnastics. Sophie, worried for his health gave the eye to the three, sibling musicians to change venue. This they did with the quieter 'Sweet Rosie O'Grady.'

The songster revellers seated themselves on any available seat, or sat with the children on the floor. They sang and supped, wives the recipients of winks and playful hugs; the cupboard love of talking beer.

The song 'Bill Bailey,' incited the robust slap of thighs and hands but was stilled by Sophie's sweet rendering of "I'll Take You Home Again Kathleen." Her voice was like a bell and never failed to move. It was only then that the reason for the celebration was remembered. Little Henry Fisher, still in his christening robes and veil, was brought into the circle. The music ceased and they lovingly watched Sophie disrobe him, and carefully put the precious christening attire to one side.

"Yer be needing them again next year Sophie," said Hannah Larkin with a twinkle in her eye.

"Don't put the mockers on me gel," said Sophie, meeting her husband's gaze. He gave the appearance of total ignorance.

The naked, plump little fellow did the rounds. Each kissed him, usually on his pink bottom, echoing loving comments, "Bless him." "Little darling." and some, though loving, of a stronger nature, usually to do with his rear end and which, Cassie knew her mother would not have approved.

Sophie Tucker sat happily down, withdrew her volumous

bosom and contentedly suckled her infant. Young Peter Fisher, whispered to his brother John, "We'll never have them John." This set Cassie wondering whether she'd 'ave 'em, but wouldn't like them as big.

'Enry's noisy gulps were stifled amid the jocular chatter and ringing laughter. Fred Lokes, who had been leaning against the window, gave a shocked cry.

"Come 'ere," he called, "take a dekko at this, the git."

A rush to the window followed, and cries of "Oh, oh, would you believe it?" and more lurid exclamations fell from their lips. Fred Lokes son-in-law, Basil Peacock and Nancy Jardine, oblivious to all around them, were in close embrace on the doorstep of 'The Cocked EYE' pub.

Eliza nudged the women, "I told yer," she said, knowingly.

They watched in silence, unbelievingly until Fred Lokes, face crimson and distorted with rage, screamed, "Come on, get 'em!"

All except Sophie tore into the street screaming obscenities, leaving the puzzled children staring, with flattened noses against the window.

Without warning, the errant couple found themselves the target of mob violence. Nancy Jardine's screams were drowned amid cries of "Whore, slut, Jezabel, give it 'er," from the outraged women. She lay, naked, cringing, bruised and bloodied beneath the colourful pub sign, 'The Cocked Eye,' her once flashy, eye-catching lace, dangled mocking, torn and muddied from the wavering, gas lamp.

Basil Peacock fared even worse. He'd put up a fight,

shouting, "Leave 'er aaht of it, leave 'er aaht of it." Two black eyes, and a bloodied nose, soon subdued him. His naked body showed all he had to offer, which wasn't much. There they lay, side by side, Nancy Jardine and Basil Peacock. The boisterous crowd grew bigger and bigger and the boos and laughter louder. Inflammatory remarks of clownish ridicule became more derisive.

"Chop it off," shouted one.

"It ain't worth it," mockingly laughed another.

"What a pity it came last," taunted a third.

So the party continued, folks pushed to get a better look and came away bent double. They leaned on window sills, doors, lamp posts, anything that could sustain their uncontrollable paroxysms of mirth.

A patrolling policeman, deaf, dumb, and blind, looked, smiled and passed on.

Cassie, trembling but caught up in the excitement, pressed her nose harder against the window-pane. Her mother would not approve, she would not tell. She saw justice not only done, but seen to be done and entered another phase in her life. A person in her own right; a me, no longer a she, a her, but an I, her own narrator.

CHAPTER 5

Before Cassie even reached the door, she knew Aunt Pol was about. Her deep, raucous voice charged every nook and cranny. Cassie greeted her politely with a kiss, which Pol returned with her usual big smacker.

"Hello cock," she said with a cunning wink, "yer mum and I is 'aving a talk, the least said."

Sam's sister was gregarious, warm and friendly. Sarah, secretly, thought her common. Among other things, she wore her husband 'Arry's cap, not just on wash days but every day. Her eyes were red with weeping, having just returned from a funeral. That the deceased was neither kith nor kin mattered not. It was her public duty to show respect for the departed, sympathy for the bereaved and fast flowing tears where the weeping was thin. Four, black-plumed horses gave this particular funeral the excellence of "a good turn aht."

Cassie's appearance gave Sarah the chance to open her mouth.

"Of course, I shall have to get permission from the school."

Pol's eyes flicked wide open with surprise; she pulled her cap forward and twisted her mouth.

"Permission?" she choked on the word, "Ya don't ask permission, ya just goes." She slid a fat finger across her bulbous nose and guffawed loudly. Cassie could see that permission was a non-goer.

Sarah stared at the ceiling and tapped her mouth like she

did at the butchers. "I don't know," she said, apprehensively.

Pol ignored the last, "Yus," she said, rising laboriously from the chair, "that's settled; I'll write awf right away."

She winked and elbowed Cassie before making her departure. "See ya later Sarah," she called.

Cassie was ecstatic. She couldn't believe her luck. The hop picking debate was finalised.

How she hated school, seven weeks leave from those old faggots.

Sarah had mixed feelings. She'd never been hop picking and never yearned to go, viewing it a place for the rough. However, the children had been peaky of late, the fresh, country air would bring colour to their cheeks. From nowhere else, she thought bitterly, would it be found. The joy on Cassie's face dispelled any doubts, instead, she allowed herself to dwell on the practical needs of the event, just eight weeks ahead.

Nearly bursting with excitement, Cassie tore from the room to share her joy with Kathy, wondering how she would last out the time. But much lay ahead. The East London schools, sports day was on the agenda and judging by the skill and enthusiasm of the competitors, promised well. The venue was Southwark Park on the opposite side of the river. Always a family day, it was greeted with special affection. So it was, on Friday morning, Sarah, Ada, Iris, her toddler and the creaky pushchair; Cassie, Jimmy, Seth and their horrible, tormenting mates, gathered to walk to Southwark Park, through Rotherhithe tunnel. The more fortunate bussed or biked but the walkers were happy with their lot.

They were a motley crowd, brandishing smiles that nearly chopped their heads in half, attired in hand-me-downs from cheeky Joe and jumble sales. Worn rubbers hung from the shoulders of the elite, much to the envy of the many who would run barefooted. Sarah sported her best, black, satin hat, cocked with a feather, lent to all and sundry for weddings, christenings and funerals. Ada's beautiful, chestnut locks were concealed beneath a floral scarf. Her amateur attempt at the modern bob had resulted in what dad called "a right cock-up." Her thoughts were with her husband, soon to beach at the pier. She leaned over the pushchair, wondering how many inches it would grow before his arrival, and whether camphorated oil would speed the process but as was her nature, she soon cast off such gloomy thoughts and entered into the spirit of the day.

Joking and laughing, they entered the dim, domed air-shaft that lay on the waters edge like a silver carbuncle. The steep, iron, spiral staircase led to the bowels of the earth and although trod many times before, its mystery remained, as did the children's curiosity and sense of adventure. The maze of cold steel rattled irritably at the noisy usurpers of its space, the hob-nailed boots, a universal insult.

The sense of adventure was heightened by the roar of heavy traffic below that gathered force with every step. With their feet firmly on the ground, they sniffed the damp, dank, musty air and cast their voices with the haunting, ghostly echoes of locked magic. Drab, blinking, yellow lamps struggled to bridge the gloom; tiny rivulets ran the blue and white tiled, domed roof and walls, trickling unsuspecting travellers. A narrow, iron-railed, raised, passenger platform ran one side of the wall. It gave a panoramic view of the tight mass of traffic below. Rickety vans, leather-clad, goggle-eyed, motor cyclists, impatient Pirate Buses jockeying for position against sullen, indifferent drivers of slow-paced horses and carts. All master, all cocky with bells, horns, honks and shout.

The troop marched in single file, with Ada leading, whilst Cassie and her mother took the rear, leaving the boys to be frog marched between. Somebody had to keep an eye on the perishers. Seth took responsibility for the picnic bag. It held a feast of bread and jam and stiff, sliced, rice pudding. The park fountain would slake their thirst and also the hidden water pistols.

In long-time fashion they sang their hearts out with songs of the day.

"Pack up all your cares and woe
Here I go, singing low
Bye - bye - blackbird."

Cheeky, passing cyclists, waved, booed or cheered, as fancy took them, more often than not accompanied with rude gestures which were returned if nobody was looking. Also, eager to impress, they showed off their aerobatic skills, by doubling over the handlebars, bringing traffic almost to a standstill and irate drivers bawling their heads off. Occasionally, the tricks rebounded on the little darlings, who returned home with the quivering announcement of, "Look mum, I've got no teeth!"

Ada's squeaky pushchair, and her mother's constant chant of "Be careful Ada," and "keep in boys," gave Cassie's behind the headache, especially as backchat was never an option.

Streamer, so called, for his proven ability to shoot a fifteen foot stream, without the aid of a box, wanted to pee. This set them all flying to their flies. But a backhander from mother miraculously shut all portholes, especially as she had donged into them all to go beforehand.

Streamer obviously couldn't wait. There he stood, his back stiff and laid back, poised, ready to defend his title, with spout channelled upon the unwary below. Another backhander turned spout to trickle just two inches from the wall. A right put down for the champion of North Block. Cassie reckoned that spouts were more trouble than their worth and mighty glad that she didn't have one.

All too soon, daylight pierced the gloom and they marched out of the tunnel serenading the streets with,

"Pack up your troubles in your old kit-bag
and smile boys smile."

Keyed up, they reached the park and stood in the queue. Much to Cassie's embarrassment, her mother relayed loudly the contents of the programme. It was then that Ada revealed that she didn't have a programme and that without a farthing between them. Giggling, she snatched mothers programme and tore it in half, keeping one half and giving mother the other, with orders to keep it folded.

Cassie nearly died but only because Miss Keyole, that prying faggot, was on the gate. With stooped head she slipped through, expecting any moment to be spliced in half. The boys thought it a huge joke. They would, they didn't have to put up with her.

Southwark Park was heaven. It had none of those 'KEEP OFF THE GRASS' signs. For one day, everybody went mad, rolling, sitting, playing and running on the soft, sweet-smelling, green carpet.

Never was a day enjoyed more; hoarse from cheering on the contestants and soaking wet from water-pistol fights, they hadn't a care in the world.

Trained from birth to oust Flat Footed Jack, their school came in the lead. Phyllis Carter and her mob lost them the three-legged race, but what could you expect from knock knees.

The Lord Mayor presented the prizes as best his huge frame would allow him to rise from the chair. Long hairs grew from his ears and his jacket stretched painfully across his belly. Mother reminded the boys to tip their caps and the girls to curtsy, with a veiled warning that she would murder anybody who laughed.

Over the moon and clutching their many prizes, they reluctantly made for home. It was hot, humid and sticky. Distant rumbles caught the ear and dark clouds swept the sky. The boys loitered, engrossed with the newly-won bat. Sarah's attempts to jolly them on, fell on deaf ears. Their hanging behinds and scuffed boots did nothing to improve her temper. Their idea of a good time was a box up with all and sundry, usually on the ground. Bugsy's black eye was living proof. Cassie thought, "What a lovely shiner." A come-uppance for calling her ginger and four-eyes. She vowed that when he swam in the river, she'd look.

Mother's voice gradually rose to screaming point but the boys took little heed. An occasional flash of lightening darted the black clouds. Earlier rumbles intensified and it began to spit. Cassie was somewhat restricted in her movements. Her arms carefully encircled a beautiful, red-roofed doll's house; never in a thousand years did she ever think she would own one. The frenzied, fork lightening zigzagged in loud, demonic rage from sky to earth. The heavens opened and the rain fell in buckets, sending everybody racing for the bus terminal. Mother's, angry, fearful voice still at it.

"Iris will get her death and only for those perishers we'd have reached the tunnel."

The severity of the storm was unbelievable. Cassie, soaked to the skin, watched in awe from the shelter of the bus depot. The red, doll's house still in close embrace, the gurgling, overworked drains bubbled streams of racing white water, flooding streets and everything in its wake.

A bus drew painfully to the curb and dropped its beleaguered passengers. They ran for shelter, the top deckers like drowned rats. The driver, the last to leave, stepped coolly from his cab. Before he could take another step, a deafening fire bolt screeched past the depot, sending its inmates reeling. A deathly silence followed.

Cassie stood, dazed, disorientated, for how long she could not tell. The soft, pitter patter of rain broke the stillness. An acrid smell of burning rubber irritated her nostrils and flaming tongues of bright light patterned walls and people alike. Through her blurred consciousness came a terrifying picture of hell. The veil lifted, she saw that the bus was a raging furnace. From beneath her feet wisps of stinking smoke curled and hurt her eyes. Looking closer, it just seemed a tangled heap. The haze from her eyes cleared and she realised with horror that the tangled mass was a human being. He lay where he had been thrown, his sightless eyes staring upwards and his body scorched beyond all recognition. She stood transfixed and watched his day's takings run a golden, molten liquid down his smouldering chest. Everything went blank.

She found herself sitting on a bench, her mother's arms around her and Jimmy. It was noisy, so noisy; bells and screams. Policemen, firemen, ambulances, shot past. The rain had ceased. The sun broke through the clouds. The doll's house lay at her feet. Ada rocked and spoke soothingly to the tearful Iris.

"Come dear, Seth will carry your doll's house." Like a zombie, Cassie took her mother's hand and together, still in shock, they moved slowly towards home, witnesses to the might of God.

Mondays were never the best of days. It was mother's wash day, also the day for the long, morning, nit picking assembly. Your hair-ribbon was the wrong colour. You were grinning when you were not. The greatest sin was to be void of a handkerchief. This presented problems for Cassie and Kathy, as their mothers were fans of the rag and bone merchant, making it a toss up as to who gets there first.

Cassie's request for rag fell on stony ground. It was piddling down and her mother was frantically searching for strong cardboard to plug Jimmy's leaking boots. She was also in a hurry to take her place at the laundry. It was a stroke of luck that Cassie's eyes fell upon John's white collar encircling the mantelpiece clock. She grabbed it and ran to call for Kathy in the flat above. She knocked and stood awhile before entering. The vigorous stirring of condensed milk in tepid tea strayed through the partially open door. The opened tin sat, centre stage, on the table. Its sticky contents ran the lid, spattering the bold, red lettering, "*Unfit for babies.*"

"Kathy's poorly today," said Edna Mannelly. "She ain't going. Come and see 'er, then ya can tell 'em she ain't swanking." She squeezed one of the four frontal metal hair curlers.

"I will that," said Cassie defiantly, moving with her to the bedroom.

Kathy was often ill. The rigours of life were not for her but she was great fun.

She sat, grey faced, propped up in a double bed of doubtful age, her night dress a worn, day frock. A length of string ran from the bent bed knob to the picture rail where a few, faded frocks dangled pathetically in the centre. Cassie thought it a splendid idea.

She reached for Kathy's hand. "You'll soon be better," she said, full of encouragement, but inwardly sad. "Uncle Jim gave me fourpence, we'll go to the flicks when you're better."

Kathy nodded weakly, "Thank you Cassie."

She left the house with a heavy heart but her natural

optimism returned when thinking of the many pranks perpetrated on that holier than thou shower. How they had raised a joint rag in response to the demeaning command, "Will you all raise your handkerchief." Hands got lost in a crowd.

The morning passed slowly. Cassie walked home to lunch, knowing that greedy Nesta would be in charge. It didn't please her. The sparse portions of jelly and custard always excused with, "I've got to save some for the others." Seth had a sneaking suspicion that Nesta was the others.

The sandwiches eaten, Seth eyed the smear of afters at the bottom of his plate, "Is that all?" he said.

"You know that I have to save some for the others," said Nesta innocently.

Cassie could see Seth's blood rising. Without more ado, he grabbed the big spoon.

"Raid her," he shouted, digging into the jelly and custard. Cassie and Jimmy followed suit, sending it in all directions. Nesta gave Seth such a clout and made to give Cassie one but was forestalled by Seth, who pinned her against the wall with the broom. Standing by Seth to the death, Cassie seized the sopping flannel and from the shelter of Seth's back sloshed her full in the chops. She threw Jimmy the greasy dishcloth to have a go, but he just sat in the corner blubbing, "I'll tell mum." Baby that he was. Nesta fought tooth and nail with a spiky umbrella she found hanging from a picture, eventually, it spiked the table leaving her defenceless. They knew that the foe had been vanquished when the bristles from the broom caught up her nose and drew blood. She ran bawling her head off to the laundry, leaving the conquerors time for a hasty retreat.

A few days later Cassie returned from school to be confronted by a tearful Nesta in the throes of a heated argument with her mother. A huge, newspaper wrapped parcel dwarfed the table.

"I'm not going," she screamed, giving it a poke.

"I cannot carry it alone," pleaded her mother.

"Then let him take it, they're his." She swore, then drew back in horror but not before her mother's hand swiped her face. The force sent her reeling. Sarah, aghast at what she had done, drew back. Nesta, clutching her red weald cheek ran sobbing from the room.

The subdued Sarah turned to Cassie.

"Open the window," she said quietly, "We'll go round the back."

Cassie dutifully drew up the sash.

"Climb out," ordered her mother, "I'll hand it over."

Cassie's heart sank. She had seen such parcels trundled through the streets before. Heard the whispers and snide remarks. Even made some herself.

Sarah sensed her anxiety, "Nobody'll see us at the back," she said kindly.

But Cassie would rather drop dead than bash into Phyllis Carter. The deserted, back lane was a bleak nowhere that housed the hospital's mortuary.

"For goodness sake don't drop it, slide it gently." Her voice had the urgency of fear.

Cassie obeyed silently and between them the ungainly

monstrosity was lowered slowly to the dusty lane. She tried to assist her mother, who seemed not to know her left leg from her right. Never had anybody made such a hash of climbing from a window. First this way and then that. It appeared in white, fleecy cotton bloomers to the knees, her skirts in uplift on the rough brickwork. It was as well the mortuary was opposite and that she couldn't see herself.

The parcel was unsightly, awkward and heavy, very heavy. Cassie pondered its contents, but sensed her mother's unwillingness to talk. Only sheer will-power and the constant plea, "Don't drop it," kept her fingers from slipping. They rested it on water-troughs, window-sills and doorways.

Never were three brass bells more welcome. They swayed in gentle tease, beckoning the feckless, the reckless, the desperate and the fortune hunter.

Staggering in through the maze of sheets, quilts and blankets, that pegged the entrance, they fell with it across the heavy oak counter.

The little, elderly, Jewish pawnbroker was haggling with a customer.

"On my life," he wheedled, his steel rims sliding his nose, "It's a fortune I'm making ya, but it's a poor man ya making me." His arms and hands moved like puppets on a string. "It's a barg'in man, I tell ya, a barg'in."

His hand clapped his head in feigned exasperation. The burly, bearded man grunted and stood tapping the table.

"Some people, I ask ya," continued Mr. Soloman.

"Yus, I'll take it," growled the customer, smacking two

pounds on the counter.

"A clever man, I tell ya, a clever man." His eyes beamed as he handed over the watch. "A man who knows... Thank you sir."

The man left without a word and Mr. Soloman turned his attention to the now bedraggled heap.

"Upon my life, Mrs. Atkins, they think I'm 'ere ter give it 'em. It's the work'ouse I'll be."

Cassie was surprised and shocked that he knew her mother but said nothing. The raffia, securing the parcel, flicked up as he snipped it, releasing the embattled paper from its last struggle.

She could scarcely believe her eyes. Father's best suit, shirts, neckties, boots and his Albert watch and chain. The clink of metal revealed further surprises, fire-irons, andirons, brass candlesticks and the mantelpiece clock. Cassie wondered how they would manage without it. A mystery bundle lay in the centre. Her mother unwound the tartan christening sash, the lace antimacassars and her beautiful hand embroidered tablecloth that bound it. She held her breath. There lay her father's mandolin.

A look of sadness came into Mr. Soloman's eyes. He had known sadness, tragedy.

"Are ya sure ya want the mandolin ter go Mrs. Atkins?"

"I am sure," she said sharply.

Cassie looked into her mother's face, and saw a woman at the end of her tether. A terrible hatred towards her father filled her being. Unwilling either to see or hear more, she moved from the counter and leaned against the dusty shelves, laden with unredeemed, heartache treasures. Opposite, a padlocked cabinet secured objects of greater value; diamond rings, gold and silver necklaces, ear-rings, bangles, brooches, cufflinks, tie pins etc. She moved closer to read the poignant inscriptions engraved on the lockets that often held pathetic twists of hair. Were they living or dead? Her imagination ran riot.

The bargaining voices overlapped, his wheedling, hers harsh, full of strain.

"The candlesticks are solid brass."

"But the sheets are worn, Mrs. Atkins, worn. On my life it's buttons I'd git for 'em."

Silence followed, Cassie left the cabinet and stood at her mother's side. The little man eyed her, then took some money from the till and smacked it on the counter.

"Take it my dear, take it," he said.

Sarah gathered up the money, "Thank you Mr. Soloman," she said quietly, "Come Cassie."

They moved swiftly through the streets, it was queer without the parcel. Sarah put an arm round her daughter. "We'll have pie and mash tonight Cassie," she said.

"And liquor mum," Cassie was hungry. Quaker oats had been on the menu for days.

"Yes dear, and liquor."

Arriving home, Louise and her boy friend Jake sat side by side on the horsehair, looking into each others eyes.

"How long have you been here?" said Sarah, abruptly to Jake.

Despite courting for ages, he showed no signs of tying the knot. Ever conscious of her own shame, she was determined to have it out with him.

"Abaht five minutes," he said curtly, grinning.

Sarah was worried; no self-respecting parent left couples alone. She looked them both in the eye, and wondered if he was telling the truth.

Far from confident, she continued. "It's about time you named the day, isn't it?"

Louise, clearly embarrassed, fiddled with her brooch. Jake brandished a grin but nothing else.

Sarah, still less confident, willed herself to take the bull by its horns.

"What are your intentions?" she blurted out.

"Intentions?" said Jake innocently, pretending not to understand, "intentions?"

Sarah's self-confidence crumbled. It was his, Sam's job to deal with it, but no, too selfish to see further than the bookmakers and The Sawdust Bar, or even to play the piano or mandolin. The three brass bells jangled her brain and fear took hold, but only for one minute before rage consumed her.

The noisy manoeuvring of the bedroom door handle momentarily defused the situation. Stooped and breathing heavily came the object of her rage. Unshaven, barefooted, tousled and decked in his shroud-like, white night-shirt, ignoring all, he tore through the room as fast as his drunken legs would carry him, on his way to the bog.

Jake burst into uncontrollable laughter. Louise and her

mother hung their heads in shame, Sarah's thoughts, those of revulsion. He had never, ever, acted in this manner before. Cassie too felt shame but it was funny and like Jake she couldn't stop laughing.

Sam, though befuddled, did not miss the look of contempt thrown at him by the last of his loins. He dangled his watery anatomy over the pan and vowed by all the ale in The Sawdust Bar to be a reformed character. He would resume Seth's piano lessons; buy Sarah a Guinness and Cassie...tears came into his eyes. What was he doing outside in his night-shirt? He shivered, the water was cold and the dash across the landing even colder. Intent upon removing his presence from his family as quickly as possible, he redoubled his unsteady steps across the living-room.

But Sarah, still fuming and desperate for Louise's welfare, had other ideas. Night-shirt or not, never would there be a more opportune time.

She clung to the door handle.

"Speak to him," she shouted. "Speak to him."

Sam had no intention of speaking to anybody. He reached for the door handle but Sarah held fast.

"Git aht me way woman," he bawled. What a tiresome woman she could be, he thought.

"You speak to him," battled Sarah.

"What abaht?" He was clearly irritated.

"His intentions, intentions." She gave Jake a glassy stare. "It's gone on long enough."

Sam pretended ignorance and tried to dislodge his wife's

hand but Sarah, back firmly against the door, gritted her teeth and with whitened knuckles held fast. Never one to use physical force on a woman, he sullenly withdrew.

"It's your place," she persisted.

He stood shivering, water trickling his feet knowing that he was cornered. He would get it over quickly.

Jake and Sam's eyes met.

"Well me lad, what abaht it then?"

It was Jake's turn to be worried. Sam Atkins had a reputation.

"It's the job Mr. Atkins, I ain't sure on it."

"Ain't ya nah, sure or not, ya ain't playing loose and fast wiv ah Louise."

"Louise and I'll talk it over Mr. Atkins." The horsehair crackled beneath his squirming bottom.

"Talk it over, did ya say? Ya do more'n talk it over mate. Ya make a date, or I'll kick ya arse through that door, faster than gunpowder can blow ya."

Sam moved near the couple and stood menacingly above Jake. Louise wept silently.

"I'll make a date as soon as I can," mumbled Jake.

"Ya make it nah. An' if she ain't as she was ya be blown even faster."

"I'll put the bans up Mr. Atkins, tomorrow."

His duty done, he shuffled into the bedroom well pleased with himself, leaving Sarah to finalise the road to the altar.

Cassie wondered if all marriages began like that. She'd not be beholden to any man, that's for sure.

Sam's vow of repentance carried to the next evening. He arrived home early, his jacket pocket spiked with the promised Guinness.

"'Ere ya are mate," he said, "git that dahn ya."

Sarah made little response. One swallow did not make a summer.

He seated himself at the piano and ran through several melodies. Cassie hung his neck, all else forgotten and raised her childish treble with his deep bass. Sarah prayed that he wouldn't ask for his mandolin. She sensed his weariness; the gnarled hands ran clumsily over the keys. The irregularity of his life had finally caught up with him.

Brushing aside the piano he withdrew, tired and weak, to the comfort of his soft feather bed. Sarah, a stickler for cleanliness, noticed with relief how clean he was, probably paid a visit to the public baths.

Cassie followed him soon afterwards but could not sleep. The church clock struck twelve. She lay wedged between Louise and Nesta in the high double bed. The flock mattress, a hand-me-down from grandma was lumpy but careful posturing eased the lumps to less sensitive parts. The heavy snoring of her father and Percy Taylor above rent the quiet, evening air. They reminded her of Uncle Jim's clapped out bagpipes and Grandad's donkey. A light shone through the crack of the door. The sewing machine wanted oiling, her mother was late tonight.

Sarah leaned over the long, dampened fire and shivered, then folded the last of the coarse aprons she had made for the hop fields. Before extinguishing the popping gas-mantle, she lit a candle, then followed the snore, tired but happy. Louise was to be married in three weeks time. She gazed upon his extended nostrils and billowing cheeks with indifference and quickly disrobed to her vest. Yearning only to sleep she slid a hand between pillow and bolster, the usual place for her night dress and drew a blank. Despite searching high and low, it could not be found. Getting colder by the minute, her temper rose. It had to be him, always pulling the bed to pieces. Without more ado, she ripped the bed clothes from him and ran her fingers down. Puzzled, she brought the candle closer, her mouth twisted and her eyes narrowed. The frilled, lace collar tucked his chin above the delicate pleated yoke. His arms lay across his chest and his gnarled hand poked grotesquely from the tight, lace, frilled waistband. She went berserk, pounced upon him and pummelled his chest with all her might.

"Get it off! Get it off!" she screamed.

His snoring ceased abruptly, he mumbled but still did not wake.

Getting little response, she swiped him viciously with her weighty bloomers.

"Get it off! Get it off!" she was hysterical.

Thinking he was at the rough end of burglars, he began to bellow oaths and flay his arms about.

"Get awwf, get owf, I'll 'ave ya."

The family, thinking they were about to witness a murder, rushed into the bedroom. They were astonished to see their mother belting the daylights out of him. When he eventually escaped from his wife, he roared with laughter, as did the rest of the family, even Sarah. But shocked at her semi-nudity, she quickly snuffed the candle and shushed them from the room. Cassie was so happy. It was many a moon since her mother and father had laughed together.

"Ya can't git it that way, turn it rahned." The strident voice of Bridie Murphy and her equally strident husband, Paddy, rose above the din of the excited hop pickers. The whole building was on the move. The stone steps echoed with heavy booted men and the soft pad of women and children.

"I'm turning it rahned," Paddy countered irritably.

"It ain't right, twist it wiv ya leg."

"I ain't a b..... corkscrew, ya silly cow."

The table like the stairs was awkward and Bridie, in common with her fellow hoppers, wasn't going anywhere without home comforts. She was near her time and eager to be on her way. It was considered lucky for a child to be born in the hop fields and she was determined to claim the birthright for her fourth. The rickety table had slipped, saved only by the bulge. Her caterwauling cries of distress brought Sam to the rescue.

"If ya don't stop that, ya 'ave it popping its 'ead ter find aht."

She relinquished the table, muttering about the in adequacies of men in general.

Cassie was agog with excitement. No more sad farewells. She ran with Kathy backwards and forwards with smaller articles to one of the ramshackle vans that blocked the lane. Sam and the boys took charge of the heavy stuff. Pol's husband 'Arry, shouted authoritative "I'm in charge," instructions, from the back of the van to the ransacking weight lifters below.

Progress was slow, achieved through fret, hilarity, impatience, comedy, an abundance of noisy shouting and sometimes cursing, but all with joint concern. Didn't all the world know the problems of loading hopping vans? If they didn't they hadn't lived.

Sarah was happy. Louise was married. She had walked the square in a borrowed white dress and a bouquet of lilies in defence of her virginity.

With these happy thoughts, she sat in the van, where 'Arry had put her, cornered on the edge of a tea chest. Cassie, Jimmy, Pol and her three children, Ossie, Elsie and Tosh, Kathy and her mother, sat on equally sorry places and waited patiently whilst 'Arry cranked the engine.

With old engines, frustration was the order of all starts. They began with a roar and finished with ph-ph-ph. It took several turns of strong, cockney arms on the handle, to set the overloaded relics into even a shudder of motivation.

Seth, whose scholarship was not to be wasted in the hop fields, stood watching. 'Arry climbed the cabin and amid cries of farewell and three false starts, lurched forward, sending the occupants sprawling all over each other, making a mockery of 'Arry's inventive order.

"Be dahn the weekend!" yelled Sam.

The van took them past the school. Cassie and Kathy

sniggered and giggled amongst themselves at the reversal of events. It was not to be a comfortable journey, only a novel experience to be enjoyed.

London seemed to go on for ever. Gradually, the traffic thinned and the van swung its way through majestic, tree-lined streets that shadowed handsome houses. To Cassie's delight, these gave way to green fields, where golden corn swayed a welcome, and apple orchards perfumed the air. Sheep bleated and munched and inquisitive cows, disturbed by the rattling irritant, raised dewy eyes and wet noses. Chickens darted the lanes and ragged, thatched cottages splashed the horizon.

Near one such lane, they stretched their cramped bodies to allow Uncle 'Arry to quench his thirst along with the leaky radiator. Eventually, they arrived at the tortuous, boulder strewn road that led to the farm. It was a test for both the vehicle and its occupants, who wondered if they were still in possession of their insides.

The cheery, burly farmer greeted them warmly, inquiring of the journey before booking them in but Pol, sharp on the mark had already staked her preference. She stood at the end of a line of huts, near the stand pipe and lavatories and cocked a thumb at 'Arry to move the van up.

Cassie peered into one of the vacant huts, which, apart from a pile of palliasses was empty. A beam of sunlight shot the tiny window and dappled the wooden floor. Here was true adventure. The arrival of more vans gave the place the look of a lively, second-hand market.

'Arry gave Paddy a hand with the rickety, old, awkward

table that would never see another move.

The convivial chatter, laughter and jovial banter were broken by the raised voice of Bridie.

"Ya never put in that box of baby fings like I told ya, ya lazy B.......!"

"Ya didn't put it aht, ya silly cah!"

"That's it, I supposed to put everything aht. Ya never look, ya all the same." Ranting and raving, she stormed into the hut, arms akimbo and reappeared brandishing a poker, intent upon bashing Paddy's brains out. The gaping crowd looked anxious but the wide grin on Paddy's face showed the extent of the threat. Well used to Bridie's volatile nature, he quickly disarmed her as though she was a child, taunting her with mock battle. Admitting defeat, she flounced back into the hut, vilifying as usual the male sex but within a short while, all would be forgiven and forgotten.

Much amused, the crowd dispersed, leaving the men to make ready their departure for home.

Cassie watched the many loud, jovial, fond farewells and saw Bridie give her husband a hug and two smackers. She felt sad that her parents never kissed each other.

With a wave of hands, gusty comments and assurances, that they'd be dahn the weekend, the grass widowers and their vans clipped the horizon.

The women gossiped among themselves before preparing the evening meal, whilst the children filled the many buckets and kettles with water, or ran to the dairy for milk and eggs.

Cassie and Kathy nervously crossed the field of cows to

the dairy, where, for a few coppers, jugs were filled to the brim with rich, yellow topped milk.

It was early to bed for all that night. They were expected to begin earning their keep in the morning.

Cassie nestled on the simple straw palliasse; it was more comfortable than the flock mattress. Each weary turn triggered the rustle of silken leaves. She was happy, oh so happy.

A chorus of bossy cockerels broke the dawn and gave true reality to her dreams. Cooing pigeons, twittering birds and mooing cows calling relief from congested udders, unlocked primitive urges, hidden beneath the trash of civilisation.

The early morning sun and the excited chatter of happy children drew her from her bed. She joined the stampede to the stand pipes and sloshed her hands and face with the invigorating, sparkling water before filling the two buckets. The ground was wet with dew, spider's webs bathed in glistening droplets, trailed the hedges.

Families sat in little circles beside their huts to breakfast and gossip. Pol dished out the porridge with a quick splodge on each tin plate and Sarah the tea, in enamel mugs. Cassie thought if gypsies lived such a life, she would be one.

The skirmish to the hop fields was a trial of strength for mothers. All, from babies to adults were kitted out in coarse, brown, sack aprons that gave the appearance of kids from a home. The able-bodied pushed or carried something and like a long, lost tribe they followed Pol with prams, carts and orange boxes, all filled with necessities for the day. Hoops of joy rose from the children and sometimes screams from deviants who tapped their mothers patience. Barring bad weather, they would pick until the late afternoon.

Cassie, Kathy, Elsie and Tosh, each battled with an orange box. Ossie, lay hidden beneath loaves and loads of bloomers and screamed.

The path to the hop fields was rough and pebbly. A few of the younger ones fell and bawled but mother's hug and warm kiss banished any hurt. The more knowledgeable ran noisily on ahead. Cassie's first view of the vines was a memorable one; row upon row of vines reaching further than the eye could see. She rubbed one between her fingers, the smell was queer, beery, but fantastic. She sat alongside her mother and Aunt Pol upon an orange box, ready to pick.

"They'll work all morning and play all the afternoon Sarah," said Pol.

She sensed Sarah's disapproval.

"It's always bin so, they won't die, earning a shilling."

Sarah did not reply, but pulled fiercely at the hops.

The women worked fast and furiously, gossiping, joking, each with a tale to tell. Cassie reckoned that she could pick as fast as the rest. The hops left an aroma and also stained the fingers. The women sang and she sang with them. How happy she was, one person's family belonged to all.

The moment of truth came when the gangling figure of the foreman came to weigh the sacks, the going rate, one and sixpence per bushel. But trouble flared when Bridie's sack hit the scales and was found to contain stones. The foreman, aware of such tricks, sullenly emptied the sack upon the ground and strode off. The tirade of abuse that followed from Bridie, nearly turned the air blue. The women were all in the throes of suppressed laughter but Pol dared to laugh outright. Cassie could hear her mother tutting but she thought it hilarious. Bridie was stupid, she should have weighted it with earth clods. The foreman ignored Bridie's protests and continued on his way, unperturbed that Paddy would have his guts for garters. She finally collapsed under the weight of her own words and slunk to the ground and with the tag of stingy B....... ringing in his ears, he left the site.

Still muttering threats, she picked herself up and gathering her children around her, proceeded to slice a bloomer. The long sharp knife took the strain off her temper. It cut deep into the loaf pressed hard against her huge bosom, any moment to deprive the coming little Murphy of its supper. The signal for the break given, mothers took up the same hazardous positions. It was bread and more bread, smeared with dripping or margarine. From then on, the older children were left to their own devises. Cassie and Kathy joined the gang and vanished to survey their surroundings.

Bridie's baby arrived that night but Cassie, steeped in the pungent infusion of the hops, heard nothing of the exciting comings and goings.

Next morning Bridie, with a smile that nigh cut her ears off, hugged her baby and held court. She lay on the feather-bed that topped the straw palliasse and regaled her luck to her many visitors.

"It's the first time I've made gels," she said to Pol and

Sarah.

"Ya lucky devil," said Pol, hovering over the baby. "Ya made a good job on it Bridie, it's never bin my luck."

Sarah kept her counsel and fussed the baby. Without doubt her babies were bonny and fanatically loved and petted.

Cassie and Kathy hung in the background eager to see the new addition.

"Come on cock," called Bridie.

They could hardly pull themselves away, nothing delighted them more than a baby.

The arrival of the cheery, blue coated midwife sent them all packing.

Sarah grabbed the milk jug and Pol the bucket.

"We'll fill 'em for ya and send ya dinner," shouted Pol. The midwife smiled, her patient would be well cared for.

Cassie wondered how long it would be before she had a baby. You had to be married. Perhaps Louise would have one.

Everybody looked forward to the arrival of the men folk at the weekend. Eager to be the first to greet them, the children made many fruitless trips to the end of the lane before their appearance.

Sarah gave the open fire a poke, then shielding her eyes from the sun's glare, scanned the distant, ambling figures. She wondered if Sam was amongst them as he had promised. To disappoint the children would be a knife in her back.

The dancing, spitting fire ran flames round the boiling, black cauldron. Pol, squatting upon a three-legged stool was busy knocking up a currant duff. Above her, a line of Ossie's grey napkins made frolic with the breeze. Nearly three, he had no intention of wasting time seated upon the hard rim of a pot, nor of listening to the murderous threats of his mother.

Pol pummelled the duff into shape, "That's it nah," she said, well pleased with herself. Reaching up, she tugged a napkin from the line, pegs and all, gave the pudding a last slap, possibly a token of what she'd like to do to Ossie and smacked it into the centre of the frayed towelling.

Paying little attention to Sarah's look of disgust, she drew the corners together with a bent nappy pin. Its unceremonious entry into the pot blotted the scene with clouds of black whirling smoke.

"Gor blimey," a voice said, "What ya trying ter do, set ya'selves alight?"

He had arrived. Cassie and Jimmy threw themselves at him. Handing his cherished mandolin to the guilty Sarah, he lifted them to squeals of laughter, shoulder high.

Clean shaven, sober, upright, he wore his redeemed clobber with a masterful air, the green and red necktie fashioned in a saucy twist.

"Ya doin' alright?" he said casually to Sarah.

"Yes," she replied, equally as casual, he would not be bothered for more.

Through the smoky haze, Sarah spied Seth. Tall and handsome, how proud she was of him. He strode towards her with a firm step. She threw her arms around him and planted a kiss upon his cheek, he appeared slightly embarrassed.

"I am so happy to see you son."

"Dad paid my fare."

"That was good." Her love voiced every syllable. He greeted Pol with an awkward peck.

"Is thats all we gits nah Seth?" she said with an amused smile.

"Uncle 'Arry's on his way aunt."

"Ee better be," she said, stirring a second steaming pot, tipped precariously aside the fire. Her one thought to give the men a good blow aht with faggot stew and duff.

They whiled the time exploring the countryside, mounted with chuckling toddlers and a following of chattering, cavorting nippers. Meanwhile, Seth and other like minded delinquents disturbed the equilibrium with a scrumping raid. The huge, red, rosy apples hung tantalisingly behind a high hedge. A weak spot was discovered. The lads climbed the heavily laden trees and threw the spoils to the girls below, who were also keeping watch. Never had they tasted such apples. The juice ran like wine with every bite. So engrossed were they, they did not see Stinker, the farmer's dog, until his snarling, barking presence ringed the trees. Seth, the last to leave, got caught in the brambles. The gang, never ones to leave a comrade in distress, pulled one end and the vicious beast the other. Fortunately, his boots were tough, and apart from bramble scratches, he remained unscathed, but the chewed boot-laces that dangled a slimy mass from Stinkers foaming muzzle, quelled any future aspirations.

The evening drew the community to the local pub, "The Red Cork." Bridie, unable to join them, lay cloistered with her lucky dip.

"Bring us a pint back cock," she called affectionately to Paddy, who immediately gave the thumbs up.

Mr Backslap, the landlord, was expecting them, as he had done for years back. He welcomed them, not exactly with open arms, he had his regulars to think of. Their boisterous ego disturbed the concentration on the dominoes, so a feigned air of sufferance kept the peace. In fact, the truth was that he relished every minute of their vibrant company, the robust singing and convivial style, a change from dominoes and grunting pigs. As for the townies, they didn't care a damn, their money was as good as the next. With the children safe in the pub garden and appeased with lemonade and buns, a good night aht was on the cards.

The place was crowded to the door, the locals on one side and the intruders the other. Sarah unused to pubs, sat awkwardly with Pol up on a dark high-backed settle, near a window, where she could see the children. The locals tutted and scowled amongst themselves, whilst the topic of their scowls joked, laughed and divorced themselves from rancour.

Sam's soothing melodies and the appearance of frothy ale amongst the dominoes, mellowed the scowlers and dampened interest for the game. Much could be shared and experiences expounded. The revellers found that windy cows and sawdust bars had much in common. The melodies gave way to the universal songs of *'The Lambeth Walk,' 'My Old Man Says Follow The Band,'* and other classics, where all inhibitions were lost in the euphoria of the occasion.

The robust singing filtered to the garden and set the children going. Cassie and Kathy peered through the window, but could see little. A thick, smoky haze hung the room. They were in charge of the little ones and felt very grown up. A game of Ring-a-roses was more in their line. Seth and his mates held sway on the picnic bench, happy in their new-found, youthful status.

The day gradually shed its light. The mean flicker from the misty windows cast eerie shadows across the garden and its youthful occupants.

Above the hullabaloo, the stentorian time-honoured command of "Time gentlemen please," rang. The rush to empty glasses stilled the clamour and the pub gradually disgorged its exuberant customers. Not to be outdone, the normally hushed lane was treated to the slurred tones of *"Nelly Dean"* and *"Dahn London Way."* The majority of the women were very restrained with their drink, just happy for a change from their humble existence, whereas the men wondered where their legs were. The mood was one of conviviality. Sam even took Sarah's arm. Cassie wheeled the sleeping Ossie, content in his warm, wet, smelly nappy. With caps askew, the locals and East Enders trod the night air together, their one thought, "to 'ave another good night aht next week."

Unfortunately, that night, the scrumping expedition took its toll. Cassie and Jimmy were doubled up in pain. Despite their frightened plea that rats roamed the lavatories at night, the fastidious Sam would have none of it and dragged them to the slatted wooden seat, where they clung to his knees for the best part of the night. He never complained and as Pol grudgingly commented, "men sometimes have their uses." He skived off down the pub with the rest of his ilk next morning, presumably to wet the baby's head, conveniently forgetting the soaking of the previous night.

Their departure, after dinner, was as turbulent as their arrival. Husbands and wives indulged in noisy displays of fond farewells or nagging rebuffs. Cassie smothered her father with kisses and again questioned her parent's lack of affection towards each other. When she married she'd kiss her man with smackers even bigger than Bridie gave Paddy. She followed her father's upright figure until he was just a speck. A retreating river, he smelt of it. Her present care-free life was fun but it did not replace the river. She stretched her hands, they were brown with picking. She smiled, left to herself she'd have thrown in a couple of clods.

The gang called her, they were off to explore the breed of the village children. The village memorial opposite the church gave a good view of them leaving Sunday school. They came out in twos and threes, then stood, stared and giggled, before progressing to rude gestures, which her gang returned double fold.

One of their lot shouted, "You've got fleas."

Such an insult could not be passed by, especially as they'd all been scalped at the clinic. With ammunition staring them in the face, it was war. The well aimed soft, golden balls, took the shine off their smug faces and doused their Sunday best as the gang continued its onslaught from one end of the village to the other. From then on it was fight or be fought.

Strange to say, it was Streamer who called the truce. Anxious to show his worth, he organised a minimum, fifteen foot, stream competition, advertising it upon the church wall. Familiar with the filth of boys, Cassie knew that it would be a big draw.

They performed upon boxes, stools, steps and benches but Streamer, seeing his title slipping away, took his stance upon a wall. Everybody watched with bated breath and gaping mouths at this life or death contest. Streamer, with tank ready to burst, shoulders and back held rigid for take off, quivered his nostrils for a good intake of breath ... then, well, he didn't ... a hot, golden ball, caught fresh in a cap, came flying through the air, spreading his only pretence to fame with a crown of golden glory. He overbalanced and disappeared from sight into the farmer's dung-heap below.

The spectators went mad with excitement and fell about laughing, doubled up with stitch, until it dawned upon the gang that the joke was on them. Never was a truce made so quickly and never a battle so royal, nor enjoyed as much, the foe vanquished for ever.

Cassie viewed the departure from the hop fields with misgivings, the river continued to tease, torment and call against the tyranny of school. She sat with Kathy in the swaying van upon a sack of potatoes and felt every knob. The receding mound of farm buildings held her attention until they dipped the horizon. A depression enveloped her, lifting only at Kathy's recall of poor Streamer's downfall. She listened to her father and Uncle 'Arry ranting on.

"On all accahnt, from what's bin said, it's the container ship and then we're aht."

"The're be a riot Sam, if that comes abaht."

"The're be a riot fer sure, but we'll still be aht, or my arse is a bloater, sold dahn the river."

Cassie had heard it all before. It was the topic of the river.

A cold, damp mist added to the tedious journey. The women were nagging. They queried the many stops to top up the leaky radiator and looked meanly at the frothy moustaches. Caught in the heavy London traffic, a pair of sweating horses nobbled the van. They shook and bobbed their heads, sending disgusting sprays of slimy, white spittle over its trapped occupants.

Nearing home, they passed the grammar school where Louise and John had been pupils. She wondered if it would ever be her luck. She had been told it was a place where you could be grown up. No, they were clever, she was not.

The haunting, distant boom of foghorns displaced all else and was as music to her ears. Mist curled, masts and funnels took ghostly shapes. Dark forms rose, foamed and disappeared, as Cassie's excitement gathered pace, each jewel forever stamped and impressed upon her brain. In her mind she shouted, "My river, it is my river." She was home.

CHAPTER 6

The smack of burning candles wafted the silent, dim landing. The pungent odour seeped from an open door, wedged with a flat iron. The tortuous wicks cast eerie shadows across the brick-walled landing, dappling the features of a young girl. She stood, her face drained of colour, before the open door. The flickering flames darted the frozen figure, as they did the many, religious artefacts cluttering the tightly curtained room; their vigil, a plain, wooden coffin resting upon a purple draped table.

With clenched fists and hesitant steps, she crossed the threshold, then paused, as if afraid. The light brought into focus the smart, gold-emblemed blazer moulding youthful womanhood. With unseeing eyes she slowly moved towards the table, paused again, then leaned over the coffin. Her shoulders heaved and her breath came in great gasps. All her pent up emotions released in gulps and sobs that racked her body. Floods of hot tears ran her cheeks, soaking the ashen face of the fourteen year old girl lying in the white cushioned casket. She lay in peaceful rest, arms folded to her breast, from whence a crucifix was tucked.

Kathy was dead. Not taken, not passed on, but dead, dead, dead. The full force of Cassie's loss overwhelmed her.

"Kathy! Kathy!" she screamed in bitter torment, "Kathy! Kathy!"

Her arms and cheeks nursed the body of her dead friend in an effort to warm the chill of death.

"Cassie," a voice said, but she neither heard nor felt the grip on her shoulder.

"Come child, she is at peace now."

She allowed her mother to lead her gently away.

"Why, Why, Why?"

Beneath the shadow of the church spire and ancient oaks, Kathy was laid to rest.

Cassie's last symbol, a handful of rough pebbles from the shore of their beloved river.

The following weeks were ones of bitter turmoil. Grief-stricken, inconsolable, she slid into deep depression. Sobs broke the night and blistering tears gauged the broken heart by day.

Sarah was worried. One such tearful day, she gently took her grieving daughter aside, enfolding her in her arms.

"Cassie," she said quietly, "death is ever with us but I trust that you will never be called upon to lose a child."

The words stung her to the quick, engulfing her in her own selfishness. That any grief could be greater than hers never entered her head. She felt humbled.

Sarah drew a batch of buns from the oven.

"Here dear, take a few of these upstairs."

Cassie, made her way slowly to the flat above and stood awhile before knocking, unconsciously expecting to hear the vigorous stirring of cups.

They fell into each others arms and Cassie found the peace and solace that had evaded her. They talked of this and that, how maybe she was watching, her face creased to that lovely smile.

Kathy's battered pencil-box rested on the mantelpiece; Mrs. Mannelly reached out and pressed it into Cassie's hand,

"She would have wished it," she whispered.

Cassie clutched the pencil-box with its worn pens, nibs, pencils and rubbers against her heart. A cherished keepsake that would top the desk at the High School where she was now fortunate enough to be a pupil and where boys were almost human. The derogatory 'four eyes' and 'ginger' were of the past and since Cassie's vision was never questioned, the horrible contraption abandoned for ever. Ginger was auburn, the envy of females and a drawing power of lecherous youth. Black-robed figures roamed halls and passages all intent on passing with patience and zeal their extraordinary knowledge.

One black-robed figure, whose sole purpose for living was embodied in the magic value of X and taught with more zeal than patience, fastened like glue to Cassie and her latest passion, Sid Halfyard. Any, who fell short of understanding in his subject, deserved to be drawn and quartered. He enjoyed the name of Snot box, as all deviants who fell over X were subjected to his disapproval with horrible, bubbly, snotty sniffs.

One particular day, he stood irate before his desk, his paunch rising and falling with anger.

"Simp," he yelled, "stand up!"

'Simp,' was a new conundrum, the class scanned the room for the unfortunate, until a threatening finger pointed in Cassie's direction. He took a book from the top of a pile and threw it at her, working his snotty drain at the same time.

"Since nothing goes in, nothing comes out," he bawled. "Two hundred lines, I must pay more attention."

Try as she may, X always evaded her, yet other subjects were a joy. At this low point, she decided to encourage the unwelcome attentions of Aubrey Crinkle, better known as Lemon-head. A great bonse waggled precariously upon a short, puny frame, any who sought conversation enjoyed it through his cap. The intensity of his passion rose to the call of poetry. This call, adorned with a bleeding heart and sent post-haste across six desks read thus:

*"Cassie dear, a thousand blazing candles
burn for you in my heart,
Light one for me and become my sweetheart."*

Unfortunately, it was intercepted by Sid who too felt the call for poetry, delivering it to Cassie with the following:

*"Cassie dear, a thousand blazing candles
burn for you in my heart"* - Aubrey.

*"Cassie dear, thems candles ain't blazing no more
in Aubrey's 'art,
Them 'bin sadly caught midfield with windy Wally's
farts"* - Sid.

Lemon-head, unaware of the debasement of his poetry, continued his advances. Cassie, too consumed with the value of X, grinned and decided to string along with him. Endowed to the status of porter, she watched him, without a qualm, bent double with her baggage. He sharpened pencils, shared his sweets, whilst she shared the X's with Sid but she balked at allowing clever clogs to accompany her home, with the admonishment that her mother was very strict. A coy brush of the golden locks aside his pimply cheek allayed his fears.

The days and weeks that followed saw Cassie and Sid wallowing in the veneration accorded only to the Epstein's of this world. Unfortunately, this close proximity kindled Aubrey's smouldering fire to a blazing furnace. He confided to her desk mate that he loved as he'd never loved before and also demanded Cassie's company to the fair. This presented difficulties as she had promised herself to Sid. Fortunately, he softened when told that three kittens were near to death and could not be left; he was a cat man.

However, it was a disaster to say the least, when he spied Sid soothing her feigned distress on the Flying Dipper.

"Hell hath no fury like a feller scorned."

A brush with a golden wisp failed to move him. In one short week, revenge saw the carpet slide from beneath her feet. A letter too was delivered to her father from Snotbox, advising him to bring his lazy, errant daughter to heel. Sam roared with laughter and banished it to the flames. He knew more than any where his daughter's talents and interests lay. Did she not accompany him on every trip?

"The daft lot. Wanna ge' their 'ands dirty. Le' 'im spend a day wiv me. That'll show 'im."

Were not Cassie's slender hands as oily as his? Her quest for knowledge of the waters surpassed any apprentice who came his way. Her ability to forecast speed and tonnage, purely from the tone of engines, even in vessels afar, was uncanny. She was a natural. He would not demean himself to reply, but

Cassie, eager to rid herself of the snivelling Snotbox, drafted her own, the gist of which was that 'She did not have a lazy bone in her body; it would also help if he showed more patience.' In other words, lay off. This was signed "Sam Atkins," by Seth.

This sent Snotbox's drain into flood, especially as Cassie was the star of the swimming gala and fêted saviour of the school.

Freed of torment, Cassie went full steam ahead with her lessons. Freed from Lemon-head's clutches, whose pimples had now risen to boils, she revelled in the admiration of men and her own sexuality. Callow youths, anxious to prove manhood, tried their luck with clumsy embrace and slimy plonkers, to be rewarded with mocking, hilarious, wrestling matches, causing ego and ardour to plummet in despair.

Realising that her high school education would enable her to escape from the drudgery and poverty which had encompassed her mother, Cassie had no intention of letting history repeat itself. She, along with many of her generation, would never allow herself to be in a position where there was not enough food to feed her children. Something had changed and it had changed for ever. One thing bugged Cassie however; terrible, migraine headaches that totally incapacitated her and on occasions, made her loose confidence.

Cassie's seventeenth birthday passed, as usual, with little notice, except for her mother's continual nag that she find a secure job, with a pension of course… and quickly! Financial security had never been her experience and at this particular moment was far from Cassie's thinking. Marine apprenticeships not available for females, she was bitterly disappointed, as was her father, though her mother was secretly glad - the river, no place for women. With these thoughts rankling her brain, she turned a corner, maybe too sharply and was felled to the ground with French Johnny and the Breton, onion vendor's bike.

"Mademoiselle," a hand reached out, "I sorry, forgives." Cassie clutched the firm, strong, weather-beaten hand.

"Sorry, forgives, je regrette."

Full of apologies he assisted her to her feet. His broken English gave a special charm, tall, lithe, mid-twenties, he oozed life. A dark, dapper moustache topped full lips, a beret dipped one eye, a red cravat wound his neck and strings of golden onions trailed his shoulders. Though a familiar figure in and around the houses and tenements and even though she had seen him pacing his bright, blue fishing-smack she had paid him little attention.

"Mademoiselle, please forgives, please? Je regrette."
She smiled, their eyes met, hers moist wells of violet-blue, his deep, concerned, dark orbs. A strange thrill ran her body.

He removed a string of onions from his shoulders and presented them to her.

Taken unawares she drew back. "No, no, it was my fault, should have looked where I was going."

"Non, non, non, s'il vous plaît?" he begged, quickly placing the garland over her head.

She returned his broad smile and in mischievous mood

made as if to take off on his bike. With one foot on the pedal he roared with laughter, not unlike her father's infectious guffaw, which she could not help but join.

He stroked her hair, "Beautiful."

Embarrassed, she made to return his gift but he stayed her hand.

"Non, non, me not hurt, je regrette." His face signalled distress.

"Thank you, thank you," she said, distancing herself from him. She continued on her way, her mind still bogged down with the frightful prospect of a job with a pension, interspersed with amusing thoughts; the romantic gift of a string of onions. Also, there was trouble at home, always something. Nesta's Breach-of-Promise case against Eddie Villars was almost due to be heard. Cassie wanted no part of it but family loyalty demanded her support. Poor Nesta had been jilted just one day before the calling of the bans. "I ain't ready for marriage," he said, but everybody knew that he had taken up with Flo Kickerwick from the whistle factory.

Nesta's, white, satin wedding-dress lay soaked in tears and tissue paper in mother's chest-of-drawers. The pink, bridesmaid dress hung from the picture-rail, its raw hem disintegrating into tangled strands like Cassie's expectations; a pathetic reminder of the fickleness of human nature. Nesta's pride and savings were in tatters. The bedroom cupboard was crammed, almost to collapse, with wedding presents. Father's flagons of ale; bought on the slate, lay, at mother's insistence under the bed, aside the rose decorated pot; a present from Pol.

Such expenditure demanded payment, with blood if necessary. But The Sawdust Bar, in its wisdom, advised caution, on the assumption that a bloke with his brains bashed out ain't likely to pay compensation.

To add insult to injury, it was also pointed out, especially to the astonished Sarah, the fact that, as Nesta was as she was, it lowered the odds.

Cassie of course was desperately sorry for Nesta but she was also angry that she allowed herself to be humiliated so. He should have been sent packing long ago with a flea in his cocky ear. The only bottom-drawer for her would be one in the bank.

In this belligerent mood and drawn by the warm, sensual smell of burning bone and tempered steel, she stopped at the farriers. A huge, chestnut Shire stood in patient acceptance, its great, shaggy hoof cradled between the leather-capped knees of the blacksmith.

She watched the rasp slate the hoof clean and the hammer slog the nails. The rhythmic beat was strangely restful. The blacksmith eased the shaggy hoof to the stone floor before becoming aware of his visitor.

"Allo," he said cheerily, "nice ter see yer. How's yer grandad? 'Eard 'ee's a poor old thing these days."

"Yes, he is none too well."

Not in the mood for further conversation, she left it at that. The truth was he was going senile.

"Yer grandad were a good'un in 'is time, an 'is father 'afore; the same 'ammer." He pointed to a heavy, deep-ridged handled hammer that lay on the massive anvil. "No man welded better.

It'll be a posh job you'll be a 'aving soon cock, I expect, as yer been ter 'igh school"

She shrugged her shoulders, it was a sore point. The mournful eyes of the Shire followed her. She patted its soft flank. Was it happy, or did it have hang-ups like her? "Cheerio," she called and made for home.

The living-room was agog with the noisy Atkins and Jameson families, all intent upon giving advice before the coming Breach-of-Promise debacle. They barely noticed her entry. She sat on the corner of the machine, the only available space. Mother's sisters, Lizzie and spinster Bella sat on the horsehair sofa, rare visitors indeed.

"I've said it once," said Bella, "and I'll say it again, she's well rid of him," she paused, "didn't I Lizzie, didn't I?"

Without waiting for Lizzie to reply, she turned to Sarah. "Look what you've had." She glared at Sam, who returned her glare with a grin.

"'Ark at the connoisseur," he mocked.

"Fussy I was, fussy," she said with pursed lips.

"An' so were they mate, so were they."

Everybody seemed to talk over Nesta's head. She began to cry, and Cassie could barely control her anger.

"Don't upset yerself cock," said Pol kindly, "there's more fish in the sea as comes 'aht on it."

"Yes," they all shouted in unison.

"It's a boy, it's a boy," shouted grandad, thinking they were celebrating a birth.

Apart from tuts of disapproval, he was largely ignored but

he continued to bang his stick on the fireguard.

"That cut-glass dish cost us a fine penny," said Bella.

"That's bin in yer cabinet fer years," said Pol.

"I know what I'm saying Pol Atkins, I'm no liar."

"An' I ain't either, Bella Jameson, so there."

"'Oo cares anyway," said Bert, "yer git it back nah."

"Yes, get it back," said Lizzie, who had a habit of repeating whatever was said.

"What yer got ter do Nesta gel, is speak aht, pile it on," said Bert.

"Pile it on," repeated Lizzie.

"It's a boy," yelled grandad once again, frantically waving his stick to the detriment of the cock's feather in Lizzie's hat.

"Someone take it awf 'im," yelled Sam.

The fracas settled, Sam returned to the subject in hand.

"Yer wanna lay it on 'ard Nesta, after all, we're all aht of pocket, especially me."

Tears ran down Nesta's cheeks. Sarah hugged her daughter and wondered if it was right to bring the case. Cassie wished it was finished with. She was sore. The corner of the machine hit the same spot as had hit the floor. Try as she may, she could not banish the dark brown eyes and firm grip of the Breton. She must be daft, no better than Nesta.

Grandad's continual fumbling with his fly buttons on the assumption that it was bedtime, sent Bella into forty fits and the rest of the family scurrying home.

"For gawd's sake Pol," called Sam, "don't take 'im."

Cassie paid little attention, her mind elsewhere. The strong hand that gripped and held, held still.

The magistrate's court was held in a dark, forbidding room in the Council Offices. "Meant to frighten the guts aht of yer," said Sam.

Long gone, scowling faces peered from dirty, cream walls. The aggrieved Atkins and Jameson's sat on ancient, brown, scuffed forms, whispering amongst themselves. Sam wore a collar and tie, presumably to impress and advance the cause. The women too, took on class with Sunday hats adorned with feathers and garlands of flowers. Even Pol forsook the cap.

Eddie Villars, villain by name and nature, sat poker-faced at the further end. His only support two highly amused, young men, a fact jumped upon by the opposing side, whose whispered vilification's rose to noisy jeers and taunts. Eddie sat tight but his two mates retaliated with rude finger gestures. The clerk's entry and signal to rise put an end to the affray. Three, black vested magistrates solemnly followed the clerk and sat upon heavy, dark chairs. The signal to sit resulted in the same disorganised banging and shuffling of feet as the previous move.

Nesta was the first witness. Visibly shaken, she confirmed, almost in a whisper, her identity, age and abode.

"I understand," said the magistrate that you are suing the said Eddie Villars, for Breach-of-Promise?"

"Yes sir," she said tearfully.

"Just how long were you engaged to Eddie Villars?"

"Two...two...two years sir."

"Did he give you an engagement ring?"

"Yes sir."

"Was a date made for the wedding?"

"Yes sir."

"And when were you jilted?"

Tears ran down Nesta's cheeks. "Three weeks... three weeks before the wedding sir." She burst into sobs.

"Sit down dear and compose yourself," the magistrate said kindly, giving Eddie a dirty look. "Three weeks aye and what reason did he give for calling off the wedding?"

"That... that... that, sir, he wasn't ready for marriage."

"He'd taken up with another girl," interrupted Sam, "he wants pole-axing."

"Enough of that," reprimanded the magistrate, looking straight through Sam.

The magistrate continued, "I understand that apart from, well, other things, it caused you considerable, unnecessary expense?"

"Yes, yes.... Sir."

"Tell me, slowly, about this expenditure."

Nesta, tearfully forgetting Sam's advice, "ter git in there and tell 'em," mumbled unintelligibly.

"The refreshments," bawled Sam, his beer in mind.

"An' all the presents, the cut-glass bowl," added Lizzie.

"Will you leave the girl to speak for herself," reprimanded the magistrate angrily.

With a little encouragement, Nesta resumed her composure and gave the magistrate more details.

Taking a deep breath, he put the final question.

"Did Eddie Villars seduce you?"

Before Nesta could answer, Sam shouted, "She is as she was."

Eddie Villars mates giggled. "Not for the want of trying, eh Eddie?" they said.

"Quiet," pleaded the magistrate, "any more interference and I shall clear the court." He repeated his question. "Did Eddie Villars seduce you?"

"No sir."

"That is all, you may stand down."

Eddie Villars took the stand with a cocky sneer upon his face. The preliminaries over, the questioning began.

"You, Eddie Villars are contesting this Breach-of-Promise case, are you not?"

"Yes sir."

"Did you promise marriage to Miss Atkins?"

Eddie hesitated, "Not really."

"Did you, or did you not Mr. Villars, yes or no?"

A hush ran through the court.

"Not that I can remember," he said cockily.

"You bought Nesta Atkins an engagement ring two years ago?"

"Yes, I bought her a ring."

"So you pledged your troth?"

"Who's he?" said Villars cheekily.

"Any rudeness young man and I will have you up for contempt of court. Yes or no, you made a date for the wedding?"

Having been brought into line, he answered in a more conciliatory tone. "They pestered me sir," he said, cocking a thumb towards the enemy.

At that point Lizzie suddenly thought of her dinner.

"Did you put the tatties in the oven Bella?" she said loud enough for the whole room to hear.

"Of course I did," answered Bella, equally as trident. "Well, I think I did... I don't know though."

"Silence in court," snapped the clerk.

The magistrate tapped his head in annoyance, "So," he said, once more addressing Eddie, "Mr. & Mrs. Atkins exercised their rights, did they?"

Eddie remained silent.

"A marriage date was fixed was it not?"

"I suppose so," he said grudgingly, "they wanted it."

"Through backing out, would you not admit that this girl and her family were put to much unnecessary turmoil and expense?"

"She'll use it some day."

"That is not for us to speculate. We have a duty to assess damages, if any. That is all, the court will adjourn."

The magistrates left to discuss the case, and tongues began to wag. Figures for damages were bandied about; one hundred guineas, one hundred and fifty, even two hundred. That "she was as she was," was secretly mouthed. "God be praised for it," but it did turn the tables, unfortunately.

Eddie Villars sat stonewalled with his thoughts. His bemused, lolling mates about as comforting as a cold bath.

The creaking of rusty hinges, grating the heavy, bruised door, silenced the speculators. The clerk signalled the court to rise, which Lizzie and Bella did painfully.

"Yer might as well be in church," moaned Lizzie.

The rest shuffled noisily and all eyes followed the three magistrate's regal entry to the three, dark chairs and awaited the order to sit.

They appeared in no hurry to deliver the verdict and after what seemed an eternity, the magistrate rose. You could hear a pin drop.

"Eddie Villars, will you please stand up," he said sternly.

Eddie Villars stood slowly to attention.

"Eddie Villars," continued his tormentor, "you have put this young lady, Nesta Atkins to considerable distress, both emotionally and financially. You will pay her the sum of seventy guineas, to be paid into this court within a week. The court is now closed." he said and left the room.

Eddie looked shocked. It had taken the wind out of his sails. He began to have doubts. She would have made a good wife. Seventy pounds, about six months wages, perhaps the club would give a loan.

The Atkins family felt that justice had been done, though somewhat meanly. All the world now knew, thought Sarah, that her girl was virtuous; nevertheless, a wedding would have been the thing.

Cassie viewed the whole affair with both disgust and amusement. A fiasco, a jester's court, Nesta had demeaned herself.

She grabbed the weeping Nesta's arm and roared with laughter. "Come on Nesta, there's a dance at The Sailor's Rest, let's shake a leg there."

"I couldn't, I couldn't," whimpered Nesta, "anyway, he might be there."

"I doubt it, he's been taken by the short and curlies. So what anyway, if he is there, flaunt yourself."

"Cassie, you are terrible."

"Of course I am. Come on, let's go to the baths first."

Nesta forced a smile but still hankered for the villain. They quickened their step. Nesta, looking neither to the left nor right, stooped with her troubles, failed to see the madly waving hand across the road. Cassie saw it. Yes, it was him, making for his boat, not an onion in sight, must have had a good day. She did not return his gesture. She tailed him with her eyes along the shingle and her heart missed a beat. A thrill ran through her. She laughed at herself and walked a little faster.

CHAPTER 7

Armed with the advice to refrain from blowing her nose too hard and always to sir and madam her betters, Cassie entered the portals of the city bowler, umbrella brigade. She knew full well that apart from the lavatory cleaner, who complained bitterly of the hit and miss of the lunchers, all else were her betters. Also, that she was of no more value than the stamp she thumped on their boring letters, loaded with finales such as: "I am your obedient servant," or some such nonsense. However, the British queue winkled out their true worth. The arrival of the red Pirate bus, topped with a Fry's Cocoa advert, obliterated the entire city gent's reserve, as with umbrellas poised, most foul, they took on the role of sumo wrestlers.

Sir, frustration at his long, awaited pension, drove a pinstriped leg to smooch Cassie's silken calf, initiating a stiletto to corkscrew his black, shiny toe and further early retirement.

Seeking change, one particular advert caught her eye: "An adaptable, young lady required for small theatre." Acting on the pretence of being proper poorly she made for Soho, the den of iniquity and tailed a long queue up a flight of rickety stairs, where, she waited, for what seemed ages to be called.

Having been called, she entered a tiny room dwarfed by a huge table behind which sat a jolly, rotund, elderly man engaged in twisting his lengthy mutton-chops. Pointing to an old, cane-bottomed chair he motioned for Cassie to be seated.

The chair creaked upon its warped legs making further movement an embarrassment, so she squeezed her bottom tight.

"Miss Atkins," he said kindly, "have you ever worked in a theatre?"

She would have lied through her teeth to escape her prison but his eyes held hers. "No sir," she said, "but give me a chance, please."

"What have you been doing?"

"Office work sir, I hate it, bored to tears."

"Theatre work is very demanding. It is hard, hard work."

"I have never been afraid of hard work sir."

"But no experience at all, I wonder."

She saw his hesitation, "I'll not let you down sir, try me."

"Well, I'll tell you something of our little troupe. We number six altogether; my wife Carmella, Candy, Lolita, Blodge, Jenko and myself Mr. Brucille, otherwise known as Joe. Our stock in trade is mostly humour, make them laugh and you are in, we hope." He laughed contagiously. "Come; meet the rest of the cast."

She followed him through musty, narrow corridors, to a room of noisy, chattering people. They ceased their chatter and eyed Cassie with kindly curiosity. She was introduced to each in turn, the voluptuous Carmella - wife of Joe; Candy and Lolita - two ex-chorus girls of doubtful age; then Blodge and Jenko - the ex-circus clowns.

"Do you think you could cope with this lot?" said Joe, playfully, cocking a thumb towards the troupe.

"I could make them a good cup of tea," she said, catching their winning smiles.

"Now money, you will be as rich or as poor as the pleasure we give. Could you be happy with that?"

"It sounds great to me Sir."

He gripped her hand. "I am sure we shall enjoy your company."

Cassie walked home on air but decided, for the time being, to keep it from the family. She smiled to herself as she pictured them all sitting round, asking about a non existent pension.

The ancient theatre was small and, peculiar to many, an old, London building, built entirely of timber. It boasted a gallery, the haunt of mischievous youths whose targets were the innocents below. Packed tightly on wooden forms they munched noisily, mostly on peanuts and toffees, scattering the floor with shucks, paper and skins with little thought for others.

Putting the wind up the audience was always a good ploy. Ear-deafening thunderstorms in misty, upturned graveyards, shrouded ghosts, unearthly screams, eerie, grabbing, whistling branches never failed to get them going.

Cassie often took the rear end of a frisky donkey and Jenko the fore. Blodge would enter and slip on the dummy dung pellets fired from its rear. Grabbing the stampeding donkey's tail they would often come adrift amongst the yelling fraternity. The downside for Cassie was Jenko's, garlic, wind ball. The transition from donkey to ostrich came not a moment too soon.

To lose favour with the audience conjured the worst of all indignities. Such was their misfortune with a sketch titled: "God save the Queen."

Cassie's artistic skill was put to a burning house where Candy, complete with crown, hung screaming from a top window, shouting, imploring: "Save me, save me."

A rescue team tore about the stage in panic and high jinks, armed with mops, brooms and buckets of water in plenty, a leaky hose and a short ladder. Many futile attempts at rescue were made. The Queen lost her crown and false teeth. The teeth were retrieved as giant sized choppers, held high for all to see and ridicule.

Rescue finally came with an undignified display of royal, bare thighs and ragged, red bloomers. The audience fell about laughing, holding their stomachs but a chance remark turned the tables, the bawdy language and laughter ceased, a strange silence followed, before the bombardment began. Boos and catcalls were followed by tomatoes, eggs, conkers, old boots, banana and orange skins, even tins. Their Queen had been insulted, they wanted their money back. Such dastardly thoughts had never even entered the minds of the players. Needless to say, that sketch was never repeated.

Home, Cassie rested in Sam's chair, Sarah sat in pensive mood on the sofa. She was worried. Her daughter had given up a good job for what? She could not even bring herself to think about it. Cassie smiled inwardly; she knew her thinking, "The wiles of men."

How was she going to tell them about Georges? Cassie

had been meeting him regularly of late but knew that her father would not appreciate her falling for a Frenchman and knew that he would embellish his nationality with cockney vigour.

Always fascinated by the river, Cassie accepted her father's invitation to join him on one of his jobs. He was overjoyed but deep within knew that their relationship was soured. The warm, loving expression of, "Dad," absent from her lips. It cut him to the quick.

She stood on the forecastle of the tug, oblivious to all and mastered the river. The cranes, barges, hoots, horns, sirens, tall-masted clippers and hell-raising funnels ignited a conflict within her, part of her grasping at the harsh, yet colourful reality of her East End existence, part of her finding it too painful and wanting to let it go. Hair thrust beneath a bright, green scarf and her lithe form concealed amongst the folds of a dark, blue, boiler suit, she followed her father over the side to the wherry and took the oars to the stricken vessel. Within minutes, they were aboard the ship. The gesticulating, Italian Skipper gave Cassie a puzzled look before leading them to the dark, dirty engine-room. To rejuvenate the clapped out engine would be a miracle but little deterred Sam, he was determined to set the struggling Skipper on his way as quickly as possible. With little to say, they interacted one with the other, Cassie's little, nimble fingers a boon in difficult places. The task complete and laden with several bottles of wine they returned to the tug. With the wind blowing in her hair, Cassie took the wheel for home.

A heavy wash to the starboard alerted her cautionary instinct. A blue fishing-smack flying the French Tricolour swung close.

"Ruddy French" said Sam, irritably, "what's 'ee up to? Think they own the place."

A young man waved from its deck, she caught her breath. It was Georges, she waved back.

Sensing Sam's annoyance, he sailed swiftly past, giving Cassie the chance to see its name, 'The Caroline.' Feeling elated and excited, her mind in a whirl, she slowly walked the dock head with her father. A solitary figure stood on the shingle. Drawing nearer, she saw that it was Georges, resplendent in a blue and white, striped, fisherman's jersey. His frame had broad shoulders, wide and protective. Her heart pounded, she stopped and felt his powerful brown arm around her shoulder.

Sam could not believe his eyes. "Cor, blind oh riley, the cheeky git. Get owf me gel." He made to prise Cassie away but she held her ground. He tried again and Georges relinquished his hold.

"Git away, git back to yer ship, or I'll break yer ruddy neck," yelled Sam, red in the face.

Cassie gritted her teeth in defiance and faced him. "Go away, go home."

"An' leave yer with 'im, that I ain't."

"No harm will come to her," said Georges gently, "I love her." He spoke with surprisingly little accent, which took Cassie by surprise.

"Love, nah is it mate, love, git owf?" His eyes blazed. He tugged at Georges. Georges shifted his stand.

"Love?" mocked Sam.

Cassie tore at her father, all pent up anger released. "Yes love," she screamed. "What do you know of love? What right have you? What have you ever done? I hate you, hate you." The vision of her mother, begging for money on bended knee before him, stamped on her brain for ever.

Sam withdrew; the vehemence of her rage shocked him. His humiliation complete, he burned with shame. She was right. "What had he done?" Walking the shingle, he wished he was dead.

Georges was more than disturbed, such words of hate horrified him and he saw a side of Cassie that had been well hidden. He had no wish to come between father and daughter.

Cassie, overcome with emotion, sobbed and sobbed. He held her racked body tightly and yearned to take her with him but she pushed him away and ran the shingle.

"Cassie," he pleaded, "tomorrow, tomorrow, see you tomorrow, at the boat."

Distraught, he watched her sink into the distance along with his early hopes, feeling guilty that he had caused such disharmony.

Cassie found her mother alone, her father drowning his sorrows in The Sawdust Bar. Pleading a headache, she vanished into the bedroom in an attempt to bring some order to her shattered nerves, feeling disturbed by the words she had uttered.

Unable to sleep, she rose with the dawn, packed a few things, left a note and money for her mother and walked out. Thinking only of her own pain and blinded to the trauma she was about to place upon her mother, she found herself alongside the river.

Georges's troubled mind also kept him from his bed; ho paced the ship, watched anxiously by Reine, his friend and partner.

Rarely shifting his gaze from the dock head, Georges caught the crunch of footsteps.

She had come, she had come.

Bursting with joy, he jumped the gangplank enfolding her in his arms and pressed her tear-stained face to his. On the narrow cabin bunk, he held her in passionate, yet innocent embrace, whispering soft words of assurance and lulled by the soothing throb of the engine the lovers fell into deep slumber.

She awoke alone, the sun's golden rays dancing her face. "Where was she?"

Slowly, the truth unfolded and fear took over. She could hear the cries of despair that would be resounding from her mother, while a drunken father sought the advice from all and sundry at The Sawdust Bar. Selfishly, she convinced herself that she had done the right thing and at this point, the sight of her lover, his face a picture of joy and pride, moving towards her, coffee in hand, dispelled all doubts. Placing the coffee near by, he gathered her to his breast.

"My darling, you slept well. I love you."

She felt the need of his care and protection. For the while, it blotted out the enormity of what she had done.

"I must go sweetheart, it is my watch, Reine must have his rest."

Lingering awhile, he kissed her on the forehead and disappeared on deck.

The squawk of greedy seagulls told her that land was near. She quickly joined Georges at the helm, where, in silent wonder, they observed the sun rise higher into a mysterious tumble of clouds.

"See my dear," said Georges, excitement in every word, "the coast of Brittany."

Cassie viewed the expanding coastline with mixed feelings. She was a long way from home. Thoughts of her family kept invading her mind like unwelcome guests. Determined to give herself some rest, Cassie hardened herself and made herself think of other things but once again fear and doubt gripped her.

"What would Monsieur and Madame Le Pioline think? A strange girl, English at that."

Little did she know that they were already aware of their son's dearest wish.

They rounded the wide St. Malo bay and hugged the coastline awhile; a sharp turn saw them gauge a narrow causeway that widened out to a small fishing village. The little harbour was tight with vessels of every description. Cassie wondered where and how they would berth. Amid the greeting calls of fellow sailors, Cassie half expected her father's voice to echo, "Git aht!"

Georges dropped anchor, with only inches to spare, alongside the granite harbour wall. All strangers aroused interest and none more so than a pretty girl. With the curiosity of close communities they took time to evaluate Georges's new fancy, noting his loving care lest her step breach the steep, harbour stairs. The old gave knowing nods, whilst the young engaged in youthful banter to be reciprocated with equal tease.

It was high tide and the low, granite gites appeared to be losing their battle with the sea.

Arms entwined, they trod higher ground to other dwellings. Her step faltered and sensing her anxiety his grip tightened, "Mama will love you," he said.

Chickens paced and scratched the seemingly barren ground, squawking irritably at the intrusion, bringing a massive, irate cockerel to their defence bearing spread wings, razor sharp beak and curled talons. Only Georges's quick intervention, with a length of driftwood, prevented a nasty accident. It withdrew, the wicked gleam in its eye speaking, "another time."

Disturbed by the commotion, a buxom middle-aged woman popped from the door of a gite that stood apart from the other cottages. A white, lace cap crowned her dark hair, and a stiff, white apron protected the long, dark skirt. With outstretched arms and gabbling rapidly in Breton she ran to greet them, kissing each on both cheeks over and over again.

"Cassie, ma mere, ma mere," whispered Georges, barely able to contain his emotions. "Mama, Cassie."

Tears ran Cassie's eyes.

Taking Cassie's hand, mama led her into the kitchen and kissing her once again placed a glass of wine before her. Her Georges was happy. Despite the heat of the day, a fire burned aside a clay oven, where Mama's loaves were baking. Mouth-watering, yeast vapours mingled with the pungent aromas escaping a bubbling pot. Sides of bacon, salt fish, a couple of hares, strings of garlic, onions and much else slung the rafters. Chickens stalked between the sacks of flour, jars, tubs, bottles and wine flagons that strew the stone-flagged floor, until a thrust from mama's foot sent them squawking on their way. A grotto of the Madonna, enhanced with flowers, ribbons and lace proclaimed pride of place in one corner, offsetting the bewildering array of kitchen utensils that hung the walls.

A short, thickset man poked his head around the door, laughing, gabbling and gesticulating he threw himself in Georges's arms.

"Cassie, mon pere, said George affectionately, drawing his beloved towards his father.

Papa held her in his gaze. "Beaux, beaux," he exclaimed, and kissed her on both cheeks.

She blushed; he laughed and patted her cheek. Mama laughed too and made the sign of the cross.

They continued talking rapidly in Breton, a form of French that Cassie found difficult to understand. Yet, strange to say she did not feel excluded. From that moment, she slipped naturally into the family. Life was sweet, as long as she did not allow herself to dwell on the pain that she had left behind. Her interest in cooking endeared her to Madame Le Pioline, as did her concern for the livestock. She fed the poultry daily, sometimes hearing herself giving them the well worn greeting of, "Watcha cock."

The weeks passed quickly but Mama's mind was on

marriage. A staunch Roman Catholic, she had her good name to uphold.

Full of ceremony, Cassie married Georges in the Catholic Church, just short of the main altar; that doubtful honour, a reservation for Catholics only. No East Enders were present; they were unaware of the marriage. It saved mum having to worry about the expense and dad drinking himself under the table, thought Cassie, trying to excuse herself, although deep down, if she would only admit it, the sweet melody of her father's mandolin and her mother wearing the hat that served the whole square would have made the day complete.

The months that followed opened a different way of life. Always busy, always seeking, always exploring. She loved its rugged people and mystical coves, yet, she remained a landlubber. Despite all entreaties, Georges refused to allow her to accompany him on his runs. Away for days and weeks, her frustration turned to anger, she missed him; she was bound to him.

"Life is hard, my precious," he wheedled, "you enjoy it here, stay with Mama."

In rebellious mood, she walked the shore, questioning his obstinacy and right to dictate her life. The constant lash of breaking waves thrilled yet gnawed at her. She swung defiantly around a jutting boulder and came face to face with a weird, dishevelled old crone, who fixed Cassie with a look of hate. It was the same person who had startled her a few days previously and then in a flash had vanished, where, she could not tell.

Returning home, she entered the paddock and was soon

surrounded by doe-eyed, young kids eager for attention. The warm, soft coats gave her troubled mind a sense of calm. Suddenly, without warning she found herself lifted upon a pair of horns. Fortunately, she landed on some bales of hay and was spared injury but who had released the bull, or mad Billy as she called him?

With Georges's next voyage her prime priority, the incident was soon forgotten. The same, determined, rebellious spirit that had led her away from home, started to overwhelm her. She would be there. She was going.

Somewhat overloaded, the Caroline sank deep into the water, every nook and cranny taken with its cargo of onions and garlic.

Cassie sat defiantly amongst the merchandise and breathed deeply the salt-sprayed air.

Georges drew his wife tenderly to his breast. "Look," he said, pointing to the wild, foaming sea-horses and then to the dark, racing, thunder clouds. "It will be rough going; I cannot take you, darling."

"Will you throw me overboard then?"

His mood turned rough and he pinioned her arms but she tossed her head and laughed and laughed in mock abandon and the troubled Georges knew that he had a wild sprite on his hands. Plagued with an uneasy mind he angrily made for the open sea.

The Caroline was a strong, stable boat, well proven in

stormy seas; the unsettled weather troubled George, not at all. The wind howled and shrieked, its mastery of the sea causing the little, blue vessel to pitch and toss, despite its heavy load. The storm broke with deafening claps of thunder; lightning ripped and forked its violent, destructive beauty to earth and sea. Waves, thirty feet high, forced the Caroline to angle almost to no return and lashed, by heavy rain, to vanish.

Caught in the mighty fury, Cassie gripped tightly on anything to hand, and for the first time ever, felt squeamish. Desperately worried for the men above, she struggled to open the hatch but fell back exhausted, unable to retain any hold.

"What if they were washed overboard?"

She heard herself shouting, "Oh God, keep them safe." This, the first time she had seriously called on the almighty since leaving home.

The boat keeled dangerously from side to side, the timbers creaked at the terrible pounding and the lamp went spinning out of control, leaving her in complete darkness. Would she hold?

"Georges, Reine," she screamed.

The vessel upended as a toy, noise, noise, loud, loud, crushing her, crushing everything. Water, water, all water, drowning and then merciful oblivion.

Someone was shouting in her ear. "Wake up, wake up." Why did they shout so? Oh so peaceful.

She opened her eyes, "Go away, go away," then slipped back into sleep.

"Cassie, Cassie, it's me Georges."

A light shone in her eyes, she opened them wide, "Georges," she mumbled weakly.

"Thank God, thank God." Tears streamed his face, the strength of his hold made her wince.

All was quiet, subdued. The sun shot its greeting through the little cabin window under which she lay.

Eager to man the pumps, he whispered "I cannot stay darling," gave her one last hug and withdrew.

The roar of energised pumps broke the silence. Sitting up she saw that the cabin was awash, bottles of every shape and size, danced, bobbed and cracked amongst sorry, damaged cases. Feeling the confines of the cabin, she clambered on deck, only to be confronted with the same mishmash of runaway bottles. The truth suddenly dawned, so this was his little game: "contraband," she laughed. Yet, even as she laughed, the face of her mother with saddened eyes, so poor, so selfless, so honest, came flooding into her mind. She dismissed it immediately.

"What price onions and garlic? A right joke." How little he knew her.

Feigning ignorance, yet feeling a sense of unease, she helped to secure and conceal the redeemable and was surprised how little was damaged. Exhausted, she slipped below to sleep but was awakened by loud, harsh voices above. Peering through the semi-gloom of the starlit night, she saw that they were aside a jetty, of sorts, whereby stood a pawing horse and cart. To further confuse, two hefty men dropped from the hatch and emptied the cabin of every sound case and bottle. Within a short while, the transfer complete, the horse, slipping and sliding under its heavy load, moved up the slimy slope into the night, whilst the Caroline sped quickly away to the open sea

Ready for answers, curiosity forced her on deck.

"Where are we Georges?" she said casually.

Pressing her face innocently to his, she whispered, "Was it a good deal?" then roared out laughing but halted, as she realised the dishonesty that had crept into her own heart. She, who, as a child had often survived the harshness of her existence by telling fibs, had now become partner to a crooked man.

"So what?" She smothered her conscience and started to giggle.

Taken by surprise, Georges looked startled, until captivated with her irresistible mirth he joined her in a roguish glee that rang throughout the boat.

Cassie had missed her family and was elated when told that they were heading for England. Shutting out the past, cruel elements they revelled in the ocean's kinder nature and relaxed in its soft, cradle rock.

The mouth of the Thames; the great arm, the fishermen's, joyous magnet of boiling, bubbling frith, never ceased to inspire her with wonder. Nearing their port of call, Reine changed course to one of the bonded tea-warehouses, where a Chinese vessel, splashed with fiery, dragons lay.

Cassie, remembered with amusement, how her brother had come home, very excited, from his job as a clerk at the docks, with tablets, bought from Chinese sailors, who promised a cure for her migraine.

Remembering her father's words of, "Git it dahn yer gel," which led to his new found knowledge, of a 'miracle cure,' being banded around The Sawdust Bar, caused her to smile. Especially, as it all came to an embarrassing, abrupt end when it was discovered that the 'miracle' had been induced by opium.

Not wanting to loose face, Sam's next words, in The Sawdust Bar, were not repeatable. Enough to say that the threat of kicked arses, floating dahn the river,' kept the neighbourhood abuzz for a week and the Chinese population running for cover.

A huge crane looped the ship, skimming the heads of the sweating dockers, oblivious to its dangers. Georges dropped the fenders and drew alongside. Little, smiling, waving, Chinese sailors ran the deck, the opium saga long forgotten.

Cassie bemused, but not shocked, followed the descent of two huge bales. Once in the Caroline, the heavy rope that bound them was slipped off and a package tied to its end. A tug on the rope signalled the hand over. Once received, the excited Chinese vanished as if they had never been.

"Tea," thought Cassie "it never was but silk, yes." Musing on these thoughts and recalling her childhood position of coppers nark, a familiar hum caught her attention, "river police."

"Move, get out, river police," she yelled.

Georges, needing no second bidding, quickly turned the boat on course, whilst Reine and Cassie concealed the bales amongst sacks of onions and sat on them. The throbbing hum grew louder and louder. "Had they seen them?" The question on her lips, she held her breath and closed her eyes. Sweating, she felt the swell of its approach, then the wash of its passing. Only then did she open her eyes to see the launch speeding ahead. They all heaved a sigh of relief and breezed on their way to their usual haunt.

They strolled to the waterfront pub, Georges eager to introduce his wife to his friend, the landlord. Like all Irish landlords, he greeted them with a pint and a short.

"My wife, Cassie," said Georges proudly.

"Ah Cassie," he said gripping her hand, "this is a pleasure. You do well Georges," he added with a twinkle in his eye.

The two indulged in deedy talk, leaving Cassie little else but to take in the noisy public bar opposite, where male dominance qualified with well aimed bulls eyes in the spittoon. A thick haze from clay pipes and strong woodbines hung the room. A quick glance sorted the neck-tied dockers from the rakish, peaked-cap lightermen, the embellished, uniformed Trinity and River Police, the white-collared tallymen and the ear-ringed sailors, all ones to tread the sawdust.

Realising that she had begun to be noticed she turned away but a familiar chuckle caught her ear. Sid Halfyard, the cheeky grin of school days still a feature, faced her across the bar. He waved and winked in a mischievous manner, she waved but gave no other form of recognition and was glad when Georges was ready to leave.

The landlord's whisper, "two a.m. at the stairs," sounded ominous.

Leaving arm in arm, they were forcefully confronted by the

drunken Sid Halfyard and his unruly mates.

Thinking they were about to be attacked, Georges hand moved to his side, revealing a glint of steel. She was shocked. The move also had not gone amiss to Sid.

"Hold on mate," he slurred. "I only want to talk with me gel."

"Let us pass please Sid," pleaded Cassie.

"Give me a kiss first," he said, leaning towards her. Cassie gripped her husband's arm, Georges let out a stream of French.

"One of them eh?" sneered Sid, "You always were a ruddy madam."

He reluctantly withdrew, allowing them passage.

"Who was that?" demanded Georges.

"Just an old school pal," she said casually, aware of his inflamed temper.

His eyes narrowed to slits, he swept her roughly into his arms. The intensity of his passion disturbed and frightened her. The force of his embrace hurt. She pulled away, his arms fell to his side. With clenched fists, he trod the highway in silence.

An eerie fog shadowed the Thames, little stirred, the seagulls long gone to rest; the haunting groan of foghorns carried the waters. Georges and Reine unleashed the wherry that trailed the Caroline, in readiness for the heavy bales of silk. The heavy weight caused it to slope perilously but with barely a sound the men dipped the oars and made for Shadwell stairs. They were smugglers. Cassie had heard tales of such escapades from her father, who always added, "If they's ever dares ter cross me path." As a child, Cassie would look at him with wide eyes, imagining all sorts of possibilities. Now, as she summed up her situation, she was horribly afraid that she may begin to find out.

Alone on the boat, she was anxious, their short absence seemed to stretch to breaking point.

The muffled splash of oars sent her to portside, all fear banished. The wherry was empty, another successful deal.

The following day, Cassie eager, yet nervous, about renewing contact with the family, held George's arm as they made for the buildings. The square was crowded with children. A group of girls skipped and sung nonsensical songs to the beat of a thick rope. Cassie, her childhood still fresh in her memory, could not resist the urge to jump the rope and sing:

"On the mountain stands a lady
Who she is I do not know.
All she wants is gold and silver
All she wants is a nice young man."

Georges stood on the sidelines and roared with laughter, then clutching her hand they weaved between balls, hoops, spinning tops, ropes, marbles and yo-yos to reach the landing.

Cassie flung the living room door open but was shocked at the torment, etched on her mother's face. Her heart ached. Had she been responsible for the brush strokes of grief on so gentle a countenance?

Sarah, totally forgiving, hugged first one and then the other, her joy unsurpassed. After all that had happened, here was her daughter, legally married and happy.

Pol, having heard, came puffing in, showing respect with Bert's new cap. Smothering them with loud smackers, she collapsed into Sam's chair, the better to embellish with tales of the living and the dead. Not a one for time-wasting she went straight in.

"Terrible it was, a box-up on poor old Mabel Tooth's grave. Yer remember 'Arry, 'er youngest Sarah?"

"Well, I don't know," said Sarah doubtfully.

"Corse yer do, 'im as couldn't keep 'is trahsers up."

Sarah tutted and Cassie smiled, she remembered him very well, a would be Romeo with buck teeth.

Pol continued, " 'Adn't been nigh the poor old gel fer years and 'ad the haudasity ter go to 'er funeral. A good turn aht it was too, no thanks ter 'im. Such a pasting they gives 'im. Black and blue 'ee was, spread-eagled on top of Mabel's coffin. God rest 'er soul."

She took a deep breath. "Yer ain't 'eard, 'ave yer Sarah? The children's party is put on 'old."

"Why is that?"

"The money in that toffee tin we 'elped collect is vanished, stolen from Wilf and Pheobe Crumplin's table, so they says. The committee ain't believing. This building ain't 'ad a robbery in my memory. Bought a new bed too, saw it come in meself. Given 'em three weeks fer that tin ter rest on their table again, 'OR ELSE.'"

Cassie knew all about "OR ELSE," having been witness to a couple of deviants from Sophie Roberts window, many moons ago.

Pol replenished her lungs with a heave of her shoulders. "Yer remember Jessie Tibbles, Cassie?"

"Yes," Cassie remembered Jessie Tibbles, always at the bottom of the class, scruffy, a pathetic creature.

"Well," said Pol, dipping her eyes, "she's pregnant, not through, well, you know," she paused and looked at Georges, not willing to continue. Leaning over Cassie and her mother, she whispered. "Mrs. Tibbles says, she got 'is feeling."

Sarah looked puzzled and Cassie burst out laughing.

"An Immaculate Conception if ever there was one."

At the point where Doris Platers growth turned into a baby, the door flung open and Sam entered. He stood gazing at his daughter, unable to speak.

Cassie hesitated, she was not sure of how he would view her but her heart overflowed as she whispered, "Dad."

His lips quivered, his eyes filled with tears, pulling his face towards hers their tears mingled.

Georges was very touched. In true French fashion, he hugged his father-in-law.

"Git awf," mumbled Sam, who always had thought the inhabitants across The Channel were a bit odd and now was utterly convinced. All he hoped was that he didn't repeat this show of affection in The Sawdust. That would be the last straw. He'd never live it down.

Ossie, a fine, strapping, fifteen year old burst into the room, Pol pulled him playfully on her lap. He laughed and twigged his mother's nose without any show of embarrassment. Pol's uninhibited love was boundless. Cassie's thoughts turned to her mother, a woman too reserved for deep, outward expression, yet possessing a stillness which was hard to fathom.

As always, on such visits, time passed quickly but tide waits for no man, so sent off with hugs and kisses they returned to the river. Sarah pressed on her daughter the beautiful, embroidered tablecloth, whilst Cassie slipped money under the mantelpiece clock, with the knowledge that her mother would be horrified if she knew of its source.

The laughter of children followed them, Cassie's eyes were moist. The East End hamlet encompassed so much dear to her heart and yet, beneath the surface, a battle was raging of immense proportions. The values that she knew to be true versus the things in life that she wanted. The poverty which could be so demeaning versus the character and strength which it could produce.

The return to Brittany was uneventful, the often ratty sea, like glass. Madame and Monsieur Le Pioline were overjoyed but a little concerned. A strange man sat in their kitchen. He was mid-forties, tall and sparse. He made it plain that he wished to speak with Georges alone. Puzzled, Georges took the man outside and returning, stated abruptly that he and Reine would, very shortly, be making another run to Amsterdam, this time, alone.

Cassie concealed her disappointment and helped load the boat with its various illicits, wondering what all the fuss was about. She then wrenched the vessel from its moorings and jumped aboard.

Georges, beside himself with anger held her in an iron

grip. "You will not, you will not," he shouted.

"Will you throw me overboard then?" she taunted.

His grip slackened and he turned away, his face distorted with rage.

Hurt, disturbed, her eyes swept the shore. She gasped, from behind a stack of lobster pots the sneering face of the queer, old woman held her gaze and then vanished. Cassie felt vulnerable, uneasy. She would tackle Georges for an answer when things were more amenable.

At the same little creek and without a word between them, they rid the vessel of its illicit cargo. Rounding Amsterdam, suspicious customs boarded them. To allay suspicion, they mounted their bikes and laden with onions and garlic traversed the streets and alleyways of the port, to sell and gossip as Johnnies have always done.

All strain gone, Cassie took the helm as she often did on return journeys but her husband brushed her aside. Thinking that he might still be a little huffed she thought no more of it.

Several miles out, a ship tipped the horizon; Georges picked up speed and drew within thirty yards of it. She was a rusty, old, Polish vessel, with the unimposing name of "Dominsky."

To her amazement Reine positioned the Oldis lamp and began to signal the vessel. Using her knowledge of the morse code, she read the returning message, "Come in, come in."

Immediately Georges and Reine slipped into the wherry and rowed furiously to the ship.

Unbelieving, she watched as an elderly couple struggled to descend a Jacob's ladder, a daunting task for the uninitiated.

They hung, clung, twisted, almost losing balance, plainly terrified, despite the assistance of the crew. Georges shinned the ladder to give further assistance. Petrified of the swell, their rescuers had little choice but to remove them forcibly to the wherry.

Cassie watched with bated breath, wondering if she was dreaming. Once safe on the Caroline, they leaned dejected and exhausted against the onion sacks. By their dishevelled appearance, they had trod rough roads.

Encouraged to go below and reinforced with steaming coffee, their sad faces creased in gratified smiles. Upon removing their sodden, worn boots, Cassie was horrified to discover their spent socks stuck fast to fetid, oozing blisters. Having bathed their feet in hot water, she scoured the cabin for footwear and in a fit of pique gave the unwelcome guest Georges's best boots. She was angry, he still had not explained himself. Her duty done, she stamped on deck.

Georges came towards her and before she could give him a piece of her mind, said, "Thank you dear, you did well."

She could not believe her ears, so laid back.

"What is going on?" she queried.

"They are German refugees, escaping persecution."

"Persecution from what?" she yelled.

"They were Jews, that's all."

"Where are you taking them?"

"To England."

"What illegal immigrants?"

"It is lucrative."

"Lucrative, flesh and blood," she screamed.

"One has to live," he retorted.

Here he was talking as though they were no more than the sacks of onions that he ferried from port to port. She was disgusted.

"And what if you get caught? It commands a prison sentence."

"Then my darling, I must not get caught." He laughed, Cassie was speechless. The whole thing repulsed her. She would leave him, jump port.

Sensing her upheaval he leaned her shoulder.

"Would you have them die?"

"But, for money, they are flesh and blood."

"I've told you, we have to live," he said abruptly.

Going below, she gazed upon the poor, lined, sleeping faces and was puzzled. She'd heard nothing. Hitler was just one of many dictators roaming the world.

"Would you have them die?"

The words stuck in her throat. She had known the welcome of her many Jewish friends at school, but with Georges, they were a commodity. Nevertheless, she would play her part in bringing them to safety.

With murder in her heart, she watched him, without a care in the world, solo fish. Grabbing several fish she vanished into the galley to vent her anger on their guts.

The fish curling in the hot fat gave her revengeful thoughts, a turn in the pan was too good for him. She pondered sarcastically what ingenious plans he had for the two, hot potatoes sitting huddled together opposite. But her musing was shattered by

Reine violently shouting down the hatch.

"Hide! Hide! Hide quickly!"

Needing no second bidding, she pushed the bewildered couple flat on the bunk and concealing them with mats, sacks and junk, sat on them, shushing them to silence.

The tramp of heavy boots and authoritative voices soon gave way to a pair of smart, navy legs. He was young and handsome and scanned the room before speaking.

"Madame," he said politely, "are you alone?"

"Yes," she answered sweetly, her heart thumping like mad.

"Madame, I am sorry, I must make a search."

Deliberately meeting his eyes, she winked cheekily. She swung her long, tanned legs in a provocative manner. He appeared embarrassed, as was meant.

Parting the makeshift, wardrobe curtains he gave a cursory glance, opened a few cupboards and full of apologies departed.

She was ashamed and angry. To save their skins she had violated herself; behaved like a tart. Delivering the traumatised couple from near suffocation she endeavoured in her limited German to allay their fears.

They wept and clung to her like children, clawing the palms of their hands. Rage and pity consumed her, what unknown terror had breached their dignity?

Georges, unconcerned, poked his head through the hatch.

"A near shave darling, you did well, a gigantic shoal is

heading this way. Come and see."

She could have hit him. She had demeaned herself, acted like a tart, yet, there he was, guilt if any, jettisoned among a shoal of fish. She stormed on deck, determined to have it out with him.

Amused by her stance, he came towards her roaring with laughter and swept her impetuously to himself, his lips pressing her pursed lips.

Entwined in his arms, and brushed by the soft spray, her angry world melted and she surrendered to the force of his passion.

Secure in their assigned berth, they were eager to be freed of the refugees. The safe house was in Whitechapel, two miles north of the river. Whilst there was less chance of detection at night on the waters, night jay-walkers ran a high risk of being stopped, questioned and searched by the police. With this in mind, twilight became the only option, the refugees could merge with homeward-bound travellers.

In the dim light of the setting sun, the wherry, the illegal immigrants and two strong oarsmen made for the shadowy Shadwell stairs, leaving Cassie to walk the heavily patrolled highway and give cover at the stairs.

Nearing the stairs, the unmistakable tread of the law could be heard behind her. Slowing down, the Constable moved to her side.

"Homeward bound?" he said.

"Yes sir," she said, meekly.

"Don't hang about then." With that, he carried on until out of sight.

The coast clear she whistled the wherry to round the pier.

The couple, used only to stepping around snorting pigs, stepped from the swaying wherry straight into the water, soaking their feet to the ankle. Leaving Georges and Cassie in charge of the refugees, Reine sped back to the Caroline.

Together they trod the humble streets of lace curtained, shoddy, little houses and tenements. Lines of washing hung dimly lit rooms, obscuring and flapping the occupants. 'Well aired clothes,' a phobia of the working class, the neglect, it was thought, would bring susceptibility to every disease under the sun.

Leaving the very poor behind, they traversed streets of bow-fronted windows and brass knockers, the homes of sea captains and Trinity personnel. Further along, they cornered the imposing London hospital tagged with the following request: 'PLEASE DO NOT USE YOUR HORN.'

The Jewish quarter was a hotchpotch of noisy, gesticulating, jolly shopkeepers who never missed a chance and whose wares often spilled the pavements; wallies, soused herrings and such like. Wistful, gentle children, intrigued with gutted chickens, squashed inquisitive noses against kosher windows, wishing it was Christmas. The Jewish speaking fraternity brought fresh hope to the illegal. Their eyes lit up and they conversed quietly in the Jewish language.

Cassie felt nothing but pity. Georges's words, flung at her

in anger, seared her soul: "Would you have them die?"

Crossing the road, they stopped before a wide, black door, studded with the emblem of the 'Star of David,' and rang the bell. The couple recognised the Jewish symbol and became excited.

The man tried to force a packet upon Georges,

"Danke sie, danke sie," he repeated but to Cassie's surprise he pushed it indignantly aside. A heavy, dark-shaven man answered the bell. Obviously expecting them, he pulled them nervously into the passage, mumbled words of thanks and banged the door shut.

Bemused at the curt dismissal, they strolled arm in arm, joking and laughing back to the river, the tensions of the past few days behind them. Little did she know that the men had committed themselves to further such missions. When enlightened, her first reaction was one of shock, then compassion, then excitement. Her whole being yearned for it. So with caution thrown to the wind and amid the threatening clouds of war, the terrorised and tortured were brought to safety.

Declaration of war found them locked in Brittany, the mercy missions blown. The weeks turned to months, and in restless, irritable mood Georges and Reine fished a little, as was permitted in inland waters and ploughed the land, whilst Cassie helped Mama, painted a little and trekked the lonely shores. Joined by Georges on one of her treks they tarried at an isolated cove and in wild abandon, lovers still, cast their clothes, swam, played and hugged, sending peals of rippling laughter across the golden sand. Eyes only for each other they left the water.

Reaching the rocks for their clothes they were dismayed to find they were not alone, the sneering face of the old crone fixed them. Then, with a wicked cackle, she disappeared from sight. A chill ran Cassie's body.

"Who is that woman, what is she to us?"

"Don't worry your pretty head, she's one of the oddities of the village."

Seeing that he was avoiding the subject, she spoke sharply, "Tell me, why us, she gives me the creeps?"

He shrugged his shoulders, "She has a thing about Grandad."

"But he's dead."

"Yes," he paused, "he was supposed to have wronged her."

"And did he?"

"Who knows, nobody talks, who cares?"

Cassie cared. She remembered the humiliation of her sister, Nesta. The pain and that awful court appearance. Even as she thought about it, a feeling of disgust came over her but she knew better than to try to convey any of this to her husband. He would just dismiss it.

"Come, I'll race you home." He took her hand and casting her cares aside, she bound the soft sand.

Mama heard their distant laughter and crossed herself. She was so happy for them but less enthused of the man who sat in her kitchen, eager for her son's company.

"Monsieur," he rose and greeted the breathless Georges affectionately, "it is a pleasure, may we talk?"

"Yes, of course, of course."

"Alone, alone, I talk alone," he said, moving towards the door.

Georges and Cassie followed; the suspicious glance he threw at Cassie was taken up by Georges.

"She is my wife," he said curtly.

He pursed and smacked his lips before speaking. "A young couple, a baby, I promise it will be the last."

Cassie felt distinctly uneasy.

"I could bring them to the Caroline at high tide tomorrow at dawn."

"Georges," cut in Cassie, "we are at war."

The man continued, "Little is happening in these waters," he paused, "a few mines, I have a chart, it will not fail you."

"Would it not be better to keep them in France?"

"The Maginot line is breached, I will say no more."

Georges and Cassie gasped, "Breached?"

"One more point," he said, "we have no money. It has been stolen. I will understand if...um."

"It matters not," interrupted Georges.

"Tomorrow then, I will deliver them at the boat." With that he walked away, leaving Cassie stunned at what they had let themselves in for.

Boarding the Caroline at dawn next morning, she had to admit that she would rather not have known. Reine's broad smile was reassuring, he had not failed them.

"They are below," he said cheerfully.

She descended slowly, ashamed of her feelings, unwilling to face her unwelcome guests.

The young refugees, a tiny baby between them, lay huddled together on the bunk, their strong, handsome Jewish features pale and drawn. A nasty gash above the man's forehead was caked with blood and the woman's hair lay matted across her shoulders, whilst the baby was saturated to its armpits with urine. Barely able to contain her emotions she scoured the cabin for towelling to ease the plight of the distressed mother and raged against her own selfishness.

Over a cup of scalding coffee, Joshua, the young husband, told in halting English a little of their experiences. She learned that they had been rounded up in the middle of the night, his wife Rebecca, heavily pregnant. The train, they were forced to travel in, was sabotaged and they made their escape. His voice broke, tears convulsed his eyes, too painful to continue. The story crept into her childhood memories, she wondered, did Mary and Joseph weep on their flight to Egypt?

It was impossible for Cassie to enjoy the beautiful summer day, the impending minefields at the Thames estuary controlled her thoughts. A merchant shipping convoy, protected by two, skirting destroyers, moved ahead. The Caroline sailed nearer the coast to avoid possible trouble, making the journey longer still. Nearing the Thames's mouth, tensions built up. With dry mouths and beating hearts Georges and Reine scrutinised the chart knowing that their lives depended upon its truth. Cassie, dumb with fear kept lookout. Nobody spoke, the three lived a lifetime through that dark patch. Once into kinder waters, the strain on the lone sailors was obvious, their bodies dripped with sweat and loud, jumbled expletives tumbled from their mouths.

The peace of the river gave the lie to war. Cranes loaded and unloaded, river traffic kept its course, sirens shrieked and horns hooted, the only concession, the grey, billowing, aircraft balloons. Cassie on the prow, stood motionless, she once more sailed her river.

A ghastly, unrelenting, ear-splitting wail carried the waters but it took Georges's strong grip to endorse the air raid warning and jolt her to reality. Looking to shore, she saw with alarm the populous running in all directions. She felt the drag of the boat, they were speeding with all haste. The deep hum of approaching aircraft turned all eyes towards the sky. The hum grew louder and louder and unbelieving, they saw objects fall from the sky. Loud explosions pierced the air. Something shaved her shoulder, hit the deck and burst into flames. Horror upon horrors they were being bombarded with incendiary bombs. Ignoring their own safety, they worked like maniacs to save their precious boat. Armed with sacks, shovels and buckets they beat, danced and stamped until their limbs felt like putty and thanked God for another pair of hands in Joshua. Shrapnel from exploding bombs flew the air, a heavy but harmless, metal object rolled the deck.

The waterfront was now a raging furnace, the bonded warehouses in flames, the heat overpowering. Police sirens screeched, ambulance and fire bells clanged and foul, acrid smoke rolled the waters, clogging nostrils and lungs. Still they came in threatening, evil drone. Would it never cease? Her family, were they safe? Ready to drop, she dare not let up. The droning ceased and within minutes the high-pitched "All Clear" rang as an angel in the night, for it was night but as light as day. Looking to shore, flames, hundreds of feet high shot the crackling air. The sky was blood red. Great teardrops ran her scorched face, her shoulders heaved with emotion, London was burning.

The last incendiary quelled, they fell exhausted on the scorched deck, not daring to go below lest an unseen, smouldering timber burst into flame. Worried for the safety of the refugees it was realised they would have to move quickly. The customs was a non-entity of falling masonry, bricks, rubble and flames, a threat no longer and so, after a period of refreshment and rest, they set out for Whitechapel, but it was a daunting task, tangled fire hoses, smoke, pipes, flooding, rubble, police, ambulances and falling buildings barred their path. Fire fighters strung high above burning buildings took their lives in their hands, others clawed the ruins for survivors, whilst some just stood, paralysed with fear. With streets blocked, detours were inevitable. A time-bombed house blew up before their very eyes, covering them with choking dust but, dulled to trauma, they were soon on their way. It seemed a never ending journey, the baby screamed and screamed. Georges took the child from Joshua's breaking arms.

"Not far now Josh," he said. No sooner had he spoken when the threatening wail of the air-raid siren blasted their ears.

"Keep going," shouted Georges, "we are almost there."

Cassie found herself caught up with a crowd of running, terrified people. The wailing siren trailed off like a run-down gramophone.

"Keep together," she called, thinking the trio were behind her. Turning, a throng of strangers faced her.

"Georges, Georges," she screamed but only the response of urgent, tramping feet. Boxed in, jostled, she stumbled on, panic stricken.

"Georges," she screamed again.

It was then that a deafening noise blanked her ears and felled her to the ground. She heard someone shout, "They've caught it," she remembered no more until she opened her eyes to a sea of gawping faces.

"Yer alright nah cock," said one, "yer caught the tail-end on it. Some poor devils 'ad it."

She was cold, a peculiar, dank smell violated her nostrils. Georges, where was he? The dim light further confused her.

"Georges, Georges," she cried.

A kindly man stood over her. "Yer safe in 'ere cock, safest place ever."

Her hand slid the floor. It was stony, cold, damp. Bewildered, she sat up and ran her hand down the wall, then quickly recoiled. She had intruded upon a ghostly, entangled curtain of age-long webs, the obscenity of which clung to her fingers. Peering closer, she gasped, shuddered and shrank back in horror. Sightless eyes, freed from vaulted, rotted wood looked down in accusing gaze. She felt sick, bombs whined and whistled. Did death matter?

"If yer 'ears 'em, they ain't for you," shouted the tin-hatted warden, conscious of his newly-found authority. A mighty explosion rocked the doubtful sanctuary, bringing down clods of earth and stone upon the hapless folk and gave an additional shake to the crumbling recesses of saints and devils who jostled amongst the living.

Cassie lay in breaks of doze and nightmare against the background of annihilating destruction. Lights, long extinguished, left an impenetrable blackness, babies and children screamed, women sobbed and prayed. The deep drone above ceased and through the silence the 'All Clear' pierced the air. The warden flung open the crypt door, letting in a shaft of morning sunlight. She followed the crowd up the steep, stone steps to the graveyard. One corner of the church was in ruins, the once beautiful, stained-glass window, gaping holes. A few of the graves had been upturned. Her mind in turmoil, battling the carnage, she made for The Star of David. They must be there, she dare not think otherwise.

Bolstered with this one thought, she ran the gauntlet of gushing water pipes, falling masonry and crackling flames. A strong smell of gas permeated the turmoil. She tripped, her knees bled but she felt nothing. The Star of David glistened in the distance, quickening her pace, she fell on the bell and pulled hard, not once but three times.

A bearded man came to the door, words stumbled from her lips. "Georges, my husband, came here last night, my Georges?"

The puzzled doorkeeper shook his head. "No, we did not

have visitors."

"But my husband, he came here."

His face registered pity, he shook his head. "I am sorry my dear, these are terrible times, try the hospital."

"Georges," she screamed, but the door closed, nobody heard.

The road to the hospital was blocked from end to end with police cars, ambulances and medical staff. Hardly believing her strength, she rushed the crowded entry and ran demented, through wards and corridors, until grabbed by the police and ushered onto the street.

With hope gone, her mind in a daze, she picked her way towards the river and the buildings. They were unscathed, at least they were safe but she did not stop. The compulsion to return to the boat drove her. It suddenly dawned, that he could be there, waiting. Hope restored, she quickened her pace but at the sight of Reine standing, wistful and alone, on the prow, her control snapped and she collapsed into floods of tears. In brotherly love, he gathered his newly found sister in his arms.

"Don't worry Cassie, Georges is tough, he will survive."

After an insufferable three hours, they returned to the hospital, where, eventually, they were directed to ward twelve.

"He's alive, alive, alive Reine," she shouted, unable to contain her excitement. Eyes darting from bed to bed, she scanned the ward, parting curtains to scrutinise the often sad unrecognisable. He was not there. She bit her lip and clasped the last, cold bedrail. Panic-stricken, she fell to the bed. It was a cruel joke.

"Cassie, Cassie," a cheeky voice called her name.

Looking up, she saw him striding the ward on crutches.

"Georges," she cried, rushing to his side. "I couldn't find you," she said tearfully.

Taking her in his arms, her joy was complete. They talked and talked, the refugees, like Georges had only superficial injuries. All were lucky to be alive.

A bell rang the end of the visit. The three clung to each other, reluctant to part.

"See you tomorrow, my darling," she whispered.

Turning to leave, they found their exit blocked by two Constables, one of whom snapped handcuffs on Reine.

"Reine Suchet and Georges Le Pioline," he droned, "you have been charged with assisting the entry of illegal immigrants. You are not obliged to say anything but whatever you say will be taken down and used in evidence."

A wheelchair swiftly appeared for Georges and they were bundled from the ward.

"Don't worry darling, all will be well," shouted Georges.

It happened so quickly, Cassie could not take it in. By the time she had made a move, they had vanished. Running into the street she caught sight of the back end of the Black Maria.

Bewildered, dejected, unable to think clearly, she involuntarily directed her feet to the last sighting of the trespassing vehicle. Heeding nothing, nobody, she walked and walked, whither, she neither knew nor cared.

Somebody caught her arm in a firm grip.

"What are you doing here?" he said.

She raised her tear-stained face and looked into the eyes of Sid Halfyard.

"Come, I'll take you 'ome," he said, placing a protective arm round her shoulders. "You're a long way from 'ome gel."

She did not answer and he said no more.

Taking charge, he eased her from doubtful paths, lifting her over floods and burdensome rubble, until, her feet squelching at every step, they came to the Atkins homestead.

Opening the door, he took a few steps into the living room.

"Mrs. Atkins, yer daugh'er," he said, then quickly left.

Cassie, all pent up emotion released, fell into her mother's arms. "They've taken him mummy, taken him to prison," she cried.

Sarah, though sad at her daughter's unhappiness, was inwardly overjoyed. They were alive when so many were dead.

"Cassie, be thankful. You still have a husband. God works in mysterious ways."

Quietly, Cassie knelt with her mother and thanked her maker, with the guilt of a child who only reaches out when in trouble.

Within a short time, she learned that Georges and Reine were imprisoned in Yorkshire and The Caroline impounded. To Cassie, Yorkshire might just as well have been the other end of the world, her domain lay within reach of the river and the wide sea.

Hoping for a quiet night, Cassie sat on one of the three

benches in the square and watched the searchlights sweep the sky. The buildings were unscathed; "A landmark," they said. Rarely did her thoughts stray far from Georges and Reine. She had been allocated a monthly visit and with this in mind decided to go to Yorkshire and find a place to live near the prison.

CHAPTER 8

The door burst open and a dumpy old woman shuffled into the dingy bed-sitter. A coarse apron reached to her toes and in her gnarled hand she held a taper, topped with a smelly paraffin rag.

"Get the matches missis," she said, moving to the fireplace. "The wind is in the right direction."

Cassie, taken by surprise remained seated.

"Come on missis with your lily-white hands, I ain't got all day," she said, spitefully.

Cassie took a box of matches from the ancient, stone-capped washstand and held them out to the old crone.

"Don't stand gawping, light it, you can see, I can't.

Unaware of Mrs. Winkle's intentions, she gingerly lit the taper and stood back in awe. The lump threw the taper up the chimney. A huge roar blasted the chimney and the fire maker moved towards the door.

"That'll do it," she said, "an' don't forget missis, the room'll need a good clean afterwards, corners an' all. The worst of that lot down there, they only do the middles."

She closed the door with such force the draught caused the falling soot to cloud the room. Black smoke billowed past the window and the acrid smell of burning soot activated all the suppressed terror of the air raids. The roar got louder and louder, the chimney breast was red hot. She was afraid. Flaming particles danced with the billowing clouds. But the fast-filling, soot encrusted hearth soon brought her to her senses. Time and again she swept the filthy mess into the bent bucket.

The hayricks, had she forgotten? No, a wily old one that. Her thoughts turned to her husband, she would be visiting him this weekend and muck or no muck she was on top of the world.

The room was covered with a horrible, tar-like substance and like Mrs. Winkle had so gleefully stated, needed a good clean. So taking the bent bucket and another crippled container she ran the length of the garden to the pump. Like everything else on the farm the pump groaned with age but with the expertise of one groomed to tricky problems she soon cajoled the reluctant handle to disgorge its sparkling, ice-cold contents.

Bending to lift the bucket she drew back alarmed and let out a scream. A lively red and green lizard swam merrily round and round.

The lump, who never seemed far away, came paddling to the well. "We get them, throw it out."

Cassie did not respond. "I can't."

"You can't?" With one deft swoop she grabbed it and threw it to the ground, at the same time giving Cassie a demeaning look.

"No guts in 'em down there, no guts at all. An' by the way missis, if you wants to use the line tomorrow you can't, because I want it. An' when you do use the washhouse don't forget to red the tiles, you never did it last time."

"Would that woman never stop yacking," thought Cassie.

Returning to her room, she rid all irritation with elbow grease whilst musing on the finer points of the farm. She loved the farm animals, the intelligent, snorting pigs, the inquisitive cows, the sheep and gentle shires. They seemed in tune with the wonderful secret within her heart.

A minute, oil stove, balancing a pan of boiling water, stood on the washstand, whilst a hissing, black kettle blocked the front of the tiny fire. Cassie dragged a small, tin bath from under the bed and tipped the boiling water from the kettle into the bath. Released from its black shutter, the little fire blazed red. Adding some cold water, she sat in the only position possible, knees to her chin. The warmth engulfed her; there were advantages in humble living.

Mrs. Winkle was at it again. She cocked her ears.

"Horace, 'ere's the soap, have you got a towel?"

A smile spread across Cassie's face, Horace, the son and heir was actually going to have a bath. She tried to imagine him standing long and skinny in the egg crock, an earthenware vessel too narrow to soak your parts. The thought of never soaking your parts horrified her. She too had been offered the egg crock but had declined, preferring to buy a bath. She recalled with amusement their surprise, try as she may to pass through unnoticed.

"You gonna drown yourself missis?"

She dressed hurriedly, dusk was falling, the bog was not a place to be after dark. The twittering scamper, that came beneath that long wooden seat, sent shivers down her spine. It was also beginning to rain, the roof could leak. So, slipping on a jacket, she ran into the yard and flung open the lavatory door, then peeled with laughter. There Horace was, a silly grin on his face, trousers straggling his ankles, shirt round his waist, protecting himself with a spiky, dilapidated umbrella.

Unable to control her mirth, she leaned the wall beside him, hysterical with laughter, then turned and fled.

"Missis."

There she was again.

"A bit of quiet tomorrow, the only day for a lie in and you goes prodding around."

Sunday, being the only day Cassie was allowed to use the kitchen oven, she rose early to prepare the food but how much noise bare feet made she could never make out, however, she had other things on her mind. How and when she could break the news of her coming little one she dare not think. It would have to be Wednesday. She was more amiable on Wednesday, Cassie helped with the cleaning.

Cassie, on her knees, scrubbing the stone-flagged floor was tired. Almost finished, she raised the soaking floor cloth and sloshed it on the floor; at the same time she felt a hot hand squeeze her bottom. Looking up, she faced Horace, a silly grin on his face. Taking this as encouragement, his grin grew wider as his hand squeezed harder. Cassie, desperately trying to suppress her laughter gave him his come-uppance with the floor cloth. He just stood there, gormless, the grin wiped from this face and the dirty, floor cloth dripping his head. Unable to contain herself further, she broke into loud laughter.

"Missis, your cocoa's ready."

She entered the kitchen giggling.

"What's the joke missis?" she said.

"Oh nothing," said Cassie, trying to keep a straight face."

"Nothing? Must be something, but there, you're all the same down there ...close."

Cassie bit into the teacake.

"Lovely," she said trying to be friendly. "You will have to teach me the art Mrs. Winkle."

"It's something when you've got to come all this way to learn how to make a teacake. If you can't make teacake, you can't make anything." She cast a withering look at Cassie but Cassie anxious not to rile her held her tongue. She had to be told, and now.

"Mrs. Winkle, I have something to tell you."

"Well, out with it then," she said, looking Cassie in the eye.

"I'm, I'm, I'm, going to have a baby," she blurted.

"Haw, haw, haw," she gave a loud guffaw, "you're not telling me anything."

This stumped Cassie, for her secret had been well guarded.

The lump continued, "Good breeders in that room, they all 'ave 'em."

Cassie felt indignant, hurt and angry. It made her deep love for Georges and her coming baby feel tainted.

"When is it then?"

"December," she said quietly.

"You'll not be confined here missis, get that straight."

"Of course not."

"A woman along the way had a breech; you could hear her screams from one end of the field to the other."

Cassie's trembling did not go unnoticed and probably thinking that she had gone too far, said, "It wouldn't happen now missis, not now."

Bursting with anger, Cassie left the room.

"Good breeders. Flaming cheek. Doesn't she know anything about love?" She felt a little strange, almost faint, soft, ethereal fluttering, like the wings of a bird stirred inside her. She sat down and passed a hand across her stomach to capture the first, gentle fluttering of human life. All anger gone, her face creased to a beautiful smile, at this wonder of wonders. She could hardly wait to tell Georges.

Feeling the need for air, she made for the stairs only to be balked by the agitated Mrs. Winkle.

"It's Rufus, the bull missis, he's got out." Dragging Cassie with her to the bedroom window they watched the confrontation between man and beast. The normally quiet animal bellowed and charged everybody and everything in its wake. The slaughter house lorry lay waiting, its sides pierced and damaged by the poor animal's fury. Clearly distraught, Mrs. Winkle sat banging her head. Not so long ago, her husband had been gored within an inch of his life. After many terrifying moments, they managed to cover its head with a sack. This quietened it sufficiently to gain hold of the rope from the nose-ring.

Mr. Winkle was much peeved, the stud licence for Rufus refused on account of it having too much of a cow's head.

Only when the bull was safely installed in the lorry did Mrs. Winkle return to her kitchen and pursue what she had left, the rendering down of pig's fat.

Cassie, pondering upon the whims of The Ministry of Agriculture and the unlucky Rufus, was suddenly stirred into action by frenzied screaming coming from below. Racing the stairs two at a time she tore into the kitchen to find one of the three oil stoves in flames and Mrs. Winkle in a state of collapse. Flames and black smoke almost ceiling high filled the room. With little thought for her own safety and using every nerve and muscle in her body she managed to heave the weighty extra large damp potato sacks that had been slung into the corner, over the flames. The remaining two stoves were red hot but desperate less they too flared she quickly turned them off, severely burning her hand into the bargain.

Ashen-faced, she sank upon the three-legged stool. The smell was vile, a mixture of rotten potatoes and stinking oil. Everywhere was black but the ancient farmhouse was saved.

The old lady, Mrs. Winkle, her face grey, was slumped almost lifeless in a chair. Cassie's arms went round her. She looked up and their eyes met. She saw the deeply engrained features, the scant, lustreless hair and gnarled, arthritic hands. "What had her life been?" A domestic skivvy before marriage and then a poor, tenant farmer's wife, worn out, still expected to toil at seventy five as she did at thirty five. Taken for granted by men, too worn and laboured themselves to appreciate her needs.

A new warmth sprang from Cassie towards her. The grey, rheumy eyes searched the young girl's face. What were her thoughts? Was it lost youth? But all she said was, "You're a good girl, missis."

The shock and strain of the fire and past events were to take their toll. Cassie miscarried and Georges was never to hear of their much longed for baby and the bitter tears that followed. Her one hope lay in the prison visit.

With sorrows cloaked and buttoned up, she was reunited with her beloved husband and Reine. They were overjoyed but she was surprised to learn that they had been pardoned and would shortly be released to take up special duties. The fact that they were so cagey about the special duties set her mind working overtime. Their knowledge of the French coast was unsurpassed and as patriotic Frenchmen with a natural quest for adventure, the Resistance movement would have been a strong draw. Though proud of them, she was also afraid but hiding her disappointment, she entered into their high spirits. They were soon reeling in their chairs with laughter, Cassie's pain over her lost baby temporarily forgotten. To feel Georges's arms around her once more was heaven. To live without him was purgatory but the appearance of the prison officer soon set her mind on its normal, common sense course, painful though it was. Barely able to pull apart, they said their goodbyes.

Not willing to stay in Yorkshire one minute longer than necessary, she decided, much to Mrs. Winkle's consternation to return home.

Next day, the train pulled out of Darlington packed with soldiers. After fourteen hours it stopped, owing to an air raid at Watford. It was the middle of the night and the station master, taking pity on Cassie, gave her a very narrow, single bed in a dark, dark room. The air raid did not frighten her, its location being London.

About five o'clock, dawn broke through the darkened room. She was awakened by rattling beds and soft speaking. Through the gloom, she made out the figures of about ten men all in various stages of undress. Totally unaware of her presence, they dressed and left for work.

"Well," mused Cassy, "Sleeping with ten men could be termed as a dubious honour." She chuckled to herself, not sure if she would relate the story back at home or not. "Aunt Pol would appreciate it though."

Arriving home, she joined the thousands of others in the munitions sheds, packing bombs. So complacent did they become that any short fall of space in the boxes, resulted in the bombs being innocently hammered in with a huge mallet.

Like the blackout and the shortages of gas, electricity and food, the constant air-raids became part of life, only lightened by the camaraderie in the air-raid shelters. Death, with its finality and no respecter of persons, was always lurking round the corner.

Desperate for letters but rarely receiving them, she became terribly frustrated and fixed with her past.

Brooding, she sat alone in the square, her thoughts, as ever, centred upon her husband and Reine. A dapper, little telegraph boy, smart in his red and navy uniform, leapt the six stairs to the square. His perky stance gave the lie to the heartache often hidden in his bag With baited breath and glued eyes she watched him pass West block and make towards her mother's North block. With sinking heart, she followed him, the loud knock, knock on her mother's door like steel bolts through her brain. From the light through the open door, she saw the passing of the envelope. Georges, Reine, Seth, John, Jim, they all came flooding her mind.

Sarah, stood motionless, the unopened telegraph in her hand.

"Cassie...it's...it's for you dear," she whispered.

With trembling hands, she not so much slit as tore open the envelope. It read: "Georges Le Pioline missing."

Shaking from head to toe she collapsed into her mother's arms.

The little telegraph lad stood obediently.

"No reply," whispered Sarah.

Neither noticed Sam's entry, now somewhat reformed, he picked up the crumpled telegram, caught his breath and left the room.

With tears running her cheeks, Sarah tried to comfort her stricken daughter.

"Georges is tough Cassie, this is not the end."

Cassie's grief was as a knife that twisted deep into her heart. By hook or crook, she would go to France and find the truth. With travel forbidden and the Caroline impounded it seemed an impossible task but not to Cassie. Always an optimist, she mulled and mulled the pros and cons until her brain almost burst. Sarah and Sam noticed with alarm their daughter's brooding silence and the hours spent, irrespective of the elements aside the charred boat. They did not understand that the wild elements, embattled Caroline and Cassie were one in suppressed anger.

CHAPTER 9

One dawn morning, Cassie, laden with essential supplies, flew the nest for the second time and made for the river. With the innocence of a blown mind, she boarded the Caroline. Damp, black, pea-souper fog damned the river and curled the boat; a gift, if ever there was one. The ominous, deep boom of the foghorns only served to increase her defiance. Lifting the fenders, she unrolled the stiff, heavy rope from its hawser and set the prisoner free. Like Cassie, almost ecstatic with joy, it bobbed and bounced with an inner turbulence. Setting the helm to starboard, the vessel spluttered, getting ready to slice through foggy waters.

"Cassie."

She heard her name, was she dreaming?

"Cassie," it came again. Turning, she came face to face with her father who pulled himself on board.

"Come on gel, let's get going," he said taking the helm.

"But dad," she uttered, relieved that he was there, the enormity of what she was about to undertake suddenly gripping her.

His heart was filled with anguish. He knew that he could not deter his daughter. All he could do was to try and make the crossing as safely as possible.

Sam longed to increase pace but the fog was thick and speed meant noise. Expecting any minute to be boarded, they continued slowly. The river seemed longer than ever, he had never realised how snake like it was before. Nearing the mouth,

Cassie's anxiety turned to dread; the minefield, had it been disturbed? Drawing the chart from the locker, they studied it until their eyes became blurred. Taking hold of themselves, they began the fateful journey. Cassie shook visibly, whilst Sam, like Georges and Reine before him, dripped sweat but his hands were firm as he manoeuvred her through the perilous waters. Once out of danger, he sank exhausted to the deck, his pallid face cupped in his hands. Cassie drew from her pocket a small bottle of brandy, he gulped twice, his pale lips slowly regaining their colour. She was worried; he was no longer a young man.

Breaking into the open sea, Cassie revelled in the choppy swell and stinging, salt spray. She felt alive. Lone vessels were few, therefore noticeable, so keeping clear of escorts they pushed ahead, often meeting the sad flotsam and jetsam of terrible submarine quarry. It was an anxious journey; submarines had little respect for size. At the first sighting of the coast of Brittany, night was falling. Passing the beautiful St. Malo bay, they made for the little fishing harbour. Caught in powerful searchlights, Cassie thanked God for the obscurity of a rough sea but that in turn, made it impossible to land. As desperation started to take hold, a little inlet, rarely used on account of its high cliff, slipped into her mind.

Sailing as near inland as possible, Sam winched the wherry. Tears straining their eyes, they clung to each other on the prow in the pitch black of the night. Then, without a word, she slipped into the wherry and was off. Sam stood motionless in the howling wind and for the first time in his life, prayed.

"Oh Lawd, she's good, brave, in yer mercy keep 'er safe."

Not fearing for his own safety, he took the helm. The searchlights flared. "Take me; take me, save 'er." In his rambling, he thought he heard her call.

Cassie, fighting mountainous seas, struggled, tipped and lost an oar. Automatically, a cry for help screamed from her lips, carried by the rushing wind, who knows where.

Thrown to the beach like a discarded stick, she lay, a soaking, crumpled heap, against the steep cliff. Digging toes and hands well into the cliff wall, Cassie willed herself to ascend. Breathing heavily, inch by inch, hands torn and bleeding, she mastered its steep terrain when, almost halfway, her fingers slipped from their pathetic hold and she fell, fortunately on to shale and sand.

Bruised and battered, her body pushed to the limit, she tried again. Looking up, a light shone into her face. Horror filled her mind; to think after all this she had been discovered. A rope dangled, teasingly before her. Wondering if she was dreaming, she reached towards it. Friend or foe, she had little choice. Within seconds, she was up the rope and standing on terra firma. A tall, hooded man drew in the rope and without saying a word vanished, giving the puzzled Cassie no time for thanks.

Diving furtively through the darkness, she reached her mother-in-law's home and wrenched the door handle but to her surprise it was locked. Shivering with cold, she tapped the closed shutters. The dog, straining his leash, barked furiously. She called quietly to him. He recognised her; she could hear the welcome of his long tail against the kennel. He whimpered, then barked again. She heard the tramp of marching boots. Hurry, please! Standing, pressed against the door, she heard the grate of pulled bolts. The door opened one inch, Cassie could see Papa's viewing eye widen with surprise. Flinging open the door, he drew her quickly in, shutting it behind her.

Falling all over her, he kissed and kissed, shouted for mama and kissed again.

Mama came trundling in and repeated the performance, babbling away in her peculiar dialect.

"Georges, Cassie, we hear nothing. He not come with you?"

Cassie felt stunned, however they had to know. "He, he,......is missing."

"Missing?"

Joy turned to sorrow, they wept and Cassie wept, her heart breaking for them. In their innocence, they did not connect Georges with the Resistance and for their own safety, Cassie did not enlighten them. She told them, in as unobtrusive manner as possible, of her flight from England to Brittany but kept the drama of the cliff secret.

She learned that terrible things happened if you broke the curfew, men simply vanished, or were shot in the square. Nearly all their animals had been taken, most families survived through barter, or rabbits caught in nets.

Cassie encouraged her in-laws to curb their excitement and keep her presence low key, until such times as she could mix with the community. Cautiously, she gradually ventured out. Taking a few eggs to a neighbour in exchange for some flour, she saw what appeared to be a foot sticking from a hedge. Investigating further, she gasped and drew back. It was the old crone who had been such a pest. Her throat slit from ear to ear. Blood gushed from her neck and toothless mouth. Pulling away, she was just in time to see a tall, gaunt man turn the corner. Feeling sick, her stomach in a whirl, she completed her errand and said nothing.

She longed to meet the Resistance but how? Madame and Monsieur Le Pioline minded their own business; they had seen too many shot in the square.

Only a small garrison of German soldiers was stationed in the fishing village. They, especially the Commandant, usually hung out at the little Cafe Solieul. She now felt sufficiently confident enough to walk past the Cafe and take note. One day, a notice in the window caught her attention.

"Waitress required."

From there, Cassie found herself waiting upon the enemy. Much to her disgust, she soon caught the eye of the Commandant. He was a handsome man. He would smile and stroke her hair upon passing. Her lack of interest only served to intensify his ardour, though polite always, he was persistent. Listening to the many conversations, she gleaned much. How grateful she was now, for the languages taught at her high school. Alderney was often mentioned, a prison mostly for Russian prisoners of war, who were usually referred to as scum and the object of cheap ridicule and rude gestures. Reports on the grapevine told of their starved, worked to death conditions.

She had often been to Alderney with Georges; a beautiful

little island, just twelve miles from the mainland. It hurt her to hear it spoken of by the Commandant as the most boring place on earth.

Walking on the only strip of beach allocated to the locals, a man, his face hidden beneath a wide brim walked quickly past her. A little way ahead, he stopped and fingered the sand, then moved quickly on almost to a run. Curious as to his motive, she stopped where he had stopped. A message had been written in the sand. "Tonight 7.30 p.m. - Cliff top."

The Resistance immediately came to mind. At last. Quivering with excitement, she rubbed the message out. Raising her eyes, the man had vanished. The cliff was the very spot where she had been so miraculously helped.

With sweating hands and a dry throat, she nervously strode the cliff top until the intended location was reached. Immediately, a hooded man jumped from the hedge and took hold of her arm.

"Don't be afraid, just follow me." He was tall and thin like the man who had helped her. His clothing rough and soiled, he could have been anybody. They walked a good distance before stopping, the path no longer a path, just prickly gorse. Peering through the gorse, the cliff was almost vertical. She heard the pounding crash of waves upon rock, bereft of the assurance of a safe shore.

The man spoke once more. "It is very steep, but I'll go first, you will be alright."

She gingerly followed him, missing her foothold a time or two but he was there. His strong, large, wide hands like a vice.

Nevertheless, the vision of them both lying dead at the bottom preyed on her mind. Would they never reach where they were going?

He suddenly turned to the right and she was surprised to see him squeeze through a hole overgrown with grass and bush. Reaching out, he pulled her through; she could hear the force of the water below. They crawled through a narrow tunnel, a dim light beckoned. Reaching the end, they came to a large cave. Scarcely believing her eyes, seated around a huge, flat stone were about twelve shadowy, hooded figures. Rising, they greeted her warmly in true French style.

"Madame, you are with friends, the French Resistance."

Her heart beat so fast she thought that she would take off. "At last, at last! Georges, Reine," she said excitedly.

"We are working on it Madame but we need your help. Reine is alive and well. Georges too is alive, we think, a captive in Alderney but we are not sure. No attempt at rescue can be mounted until we are sure."

Cassie's heart sank at the thought of Georges captive in Alderney.

"He has of course a false identity." He handed her a paper. "There it is written down, memorise it."

She took the paper, read it and committed it to memory.

He continued, "The Commandant, you know him?"

"Only to serve coffee."

"Of course, of course. He's taken a shine to you. He has Alderney in his hands."

She sensed his meaning; Georges ever before her.

"It, it, it would not be difficult." He was hesitant.

She sat in silence with pursed lips. The Commandant's gloating face sickened her but for Georges, anything. She nodded.

"Good, we shall not desert you. Come let's take a cup together. He filled the cups and raising them high in defiant voice, they drank to Georges and Vive la France.

"You cannot leave tonight Madame, the curfew."

Overjoyed to be part of the Resistance she put all thoughts of the Commandant behind her, spent a wonderful evening and slept peacefully, the first time for months. Next morning, the euphoria dimmed a little under the weight of what was expected of her. A rope had been dropped from above to make her descent easier. With fond farewells, she made her exit, still without knowledge of her confederates.

From then on, her days in the cafe took on a new meaning. When serving the Commandant's coffee she returned his smile but to avoid suspicion she sometimes allowed others to serve him. It was then she noticed his annoyance. His approach became bolder in the squeeze of her hand. One day, lingering a little too long at the mention of Alderney, he pulled her towards him to request that he partner her at the dance. She agreed, eventually becoming part of his life, enduring the whiplash of his passion, but with clever manoeuvring avoiding the ultimate. Despite this, she made little headway towards her goal. The disappointment and frustration became unbearable.

Meanwhile, she was to experience the barbs of local anger at her fraternisation. Mama and papa were devastated. "What loyalty is this?"

Unable to confide in them for security reasons, lest they were pulled in, she decided to leave the homestead, as soon as able, to save them future hurt and harassment. Where to go she had not a clue. The Commandant aware of the situation offered her the protection of his villa. Desperate, through lack of information and worn mentally by vicious taunts, she was tempted to accept but the whole idea repulsed her.

An incident in the village Fore Street, one day, induced her to change her mind. Leaving the café, she found herself surrounded by a group of snarling people baying for her blood.

"The dirty whore," said one, "the Commandant's bit." "Lynch her, over the cliff."

Cassie had never experienced such horror.

"Strip her first, the dirty cow. Get rid of those locks he loves to stroke."

They rushed her. She felt their hands pulling at her clothing nearly breaking her arms. Great chunks of her hair fell to the ground. She stood naked, tears running her cheeks. The men gloating.

"Come on, over now."

Just when she thought her last moment had come, a voice shouted "Stop, stop, stop!"

A tall man pushed angrily through the crowd.

The mob withdrew.

"Are you mad, do you want the whole village sacrificed?

She's not worth it, the slut. You've had your way, let the bitch go. Our time will come." He punched the air, "Vive la France."

"Vive la France," they echoed.

Leaving Cassie naked, shaken, scratched and humiliated they gradually dispersed, hatred written all over their faces. Hiding her nakedness with a few rags she limped home to be met with bland, bewildered, cold faces.

"How could you do this to us, to our poor boy?" Madame Le Pioline, crossing herself repeated two Hail Mary's and shunted out of the room, leaving Cassie to dress decently and pack her few bits.

Having no other option she made for the villa. Shocked at her plight, and genuinely concerned, he held her lovingly in his arms, further inciting Cassie to boil him in oil. Yet, strange to say, resting awhile against his sturdy body she drew comfort. Almost at the end of her tether, she wondered how much further she could go and if put to the test, could she win?

"We have a nice little apartment upstairs, you must rest."

Allowing him the lead, she fell upon his protection.

"You will be safe here, I will protect you."

Left alone, Cassie fell on to the bed. Sleep did not come easily and when it did it was punctuated with horrific dreams. She was back to her childhood but this time her nose was not pressed up against the window watching the rough justice of the East End. She was the victim, being dragged through the streets with sounds of "Whore, slut, Jezebel, give it 'er."

A faint voice echoed in the background. "Leave 'er aaht of it."

As consciousness returned, Cassie realised that the reality of her wakeful hours, equalled the turmoil of her dreams.

Every evening, dressed in his expensive presents, Cassie had to respond to his affection. She felt sick, but dare not pull away.

In his almost perfect French, he would confide and open out his heart. Exalting her worth and what a difference she made to his mundane life.

Over dinner, she sat quietly by his side, feigning ignorance of the German language but listening to every word, her German now at its peak.

She caught her breath, they were talking about Alderney.

"It's the last place on hell I want to go but shall have to put in an appearance."

Here was the opening she had longed for but how, without giving herself away, could she follow it up?

She sat, her ears cocked but to her bitter disappointment, the conversation petered out to nothing.

An opportunity presented itself that evening.

"My darling," he said upon leaving, "I shall not be around tomorrow; my staff will take care of you. Do not go beyond the confines of the gardens.

"Oh Hans, I shall miss you, must you go, will it be all day?" she said pouting, kissing his lips and hating herself.

"I'm afraid so sweetheart, duty calls me to that wretched place."

"What wretched place?"

"Alderney, that wilderness."

Teasingly, she sidled up to him. "I'd like to come with you; then you won't get so fed up with the whole occasion."

"You little monkey," he laughed, flattered at the attention, "I'll think about it."

"Can't see a problem, myself," giggled Cassie

"Okay then, tomorrow at nine, but you will be bored."

Kissing her goodnight, he left the room. She almost danced for joy and could not believe her luck.

Sleep evaded her that night, thoughts turning over and over again in her mind. She must not fail.

Seated on the boat next morning, Cassie's brain was so clamped up that she failed to notice the Commandant squeezing her body and whispering in her ear. It seemed all too short a journey, too quick for the task ahead. Telling herself that she was no shirker, she stepped ashore by his side, to be met by a platoon of clicking-heeled guards.

Taking her arm, he led her to the only imposing building on the island. Directing her to a large room, he bid her be seated whilst he engaged himself with the wall to wall cabinets. Germans were sticklers for perfection and order. If Georges was held there, his name would be too.

Gazing through the window, she noticed columns of men, if you could call them men, barely able to walk, hustled by German guards. Dejected, thin, ragged, looking neither to the left nor to the right, they shuffled along obediently, like living scarecrows. Shocked, her blood ran cold. Was Georges among them? How could men treat men so?

"Who are those men Hans?" she enquired.

"Don't you worry your pretty head with that scum. They are stupid, like their Russian names." He took a sheet from the file and spat on it. "Look at it, who can read that?"

As she rose from her seat a soldier knocked. Leaving the cabinet open, he answered the door and read the letter. The letter evidently irritated him. He appeared angry.

"Can't they do anything on their own?" With that, he left the room and Cassie made a dive for the cabinet. Her hands trembled. A large photograph of Hitler looked menacingly down. Not knowing where to look, she pulled open a small file.

Immediately, the heading caught her eye. "French prisoners."

Fingers all sixes and sevens she tore through its pages. Sure enough, Georges's false identity name and number of hut stared at her. She nearly fainted.

At that moment, the Commandant burst into the room. He looked surprised. "My dear, whatever are you doing?"

Hardly able to control her thumping heart, she laughed coarsely and replaced the file. "Their Russian names, they mesmerise me, however do you pronounce them?"

"I don't," he said, locking the cabinets.

Cassie showered him with kisses, he responded passionately. She was a minx, sometimes aloof, other times smouldering with passion.

"I have a meeting this afternoon my dear. After lunch, you will have to amuse yourself. I told you it was boring."

"Oh, don't worry about me. I'll take a walk round. The

seals are very amusing."

"It will be the only amusement in this place."

Wandering the Island, apart from explosions from a distant quarry, it could not have been more peaceful. The sudden outbursts intrigued her. She followed her ears and came upon heavy machinery, digging what appeared to be bunkers beneath the earth. Not wishing to attract attention she looked from a distance. Scores of malnourished, demoralised men lugged heavy tools around; their dust-filled, sunken eyes, never shifting from the task ahead. Another terrific explosion shook the ground beneath her. About a couple of dozen men scrambled from the bunker, so weak they could hardly stand. That they had received a terrific pounding was easy to see. Caked with filth they struggled to their feet, helped with the butt end of rifles.

Could Georges be amongst them? Were her eyes playing tricks? No, twisting around to get a better hold his expressionless face came within her gaze. He looked but only with demoralised, unseeing eyes. Almost mad with frustration, she tried everything imaginable to draw his attention. Then, yes, the first glint of a smile moved his sunken cheeks. Like lightning, she tapped the morse code out on her thigh.

"Be prepared, help coming." She could tell he understood but he showed no surprise, his training still a calling. Dragging his rag-bound feet, he again entered the bunker still spewing dirt and dust.

Cassie wept silently. If he was not rescued soon he would be dead. At least she had given him hope, if nothing else. With the aid of the Commandant's readily bestowed chit, she was able to tour the garrison and camp at will. She made mental notes of the huts, especially the number of Georges's hut. Also the proximity and quality of the beaches nearest the huts. Carrying all this in her mind, she returned to the point of departure.

The Commandant greeted her affectionately, full of apologies for his absence. Walking the shore to board the boat, she frivolously questioned him.

"Hans darling, whatever do you need all those huts for?"

"To let the lazy trash sleep," then craftily added "sometimes."

She felt choked, but sidled up to him.

The German garrison was an occupying force with little to do. Drink readily available, boredom was relieved with the weekly bash, where they often drank themselves into oblivion. Communication with the Resistance was through a secret place in the churchyard bordering the Catholic Church. The Resistance decided to take advantage of such a night for the rescue.

Cassie sat on the edge of the bed, her mind in a whirl, the fateful evening upon her. A determined knock on the door pulled her jumbled thoughts together. Opening the door, her tormentor faced her, a sickening smile upon his face. A visit before dinner was normal to unburden himself and give demonstrations of his affection, which seemed to get more passionate each day but what could she expect, she thought bitterly from her provocative behaviour? Without his usual small-talk, his great arms pinioned her to his breast, breathing heavily. She felt that she was going mad.

"No, no, please."

"Come on, come on, don't be such a little prude."

Only a knock on the door saved her.

"Blast them, blast them," he roared. Rising, his face red with anger, he answered the door and literally tore the envelope from the soldiers hand. Banging the door, he left without a word.

Lifting herself off the bed, she trembled and shook with fright but somehow, she had to go on. "Dear Lord, no more please."

Dinner was as normal. Cassie bright and cheerful, giving the impression that she had forgotten and forgiven his little indiscretion.

Lifting her glass, joining in the noisy carousal she pretended to have a whale of a time, until they dropped in drunken stupor off their chairs. Returning quickly to her room, she flung off the expensive dress and donning rough clothes left the villa for ever.

Creeping, crawling, tiptoeing, walking, running in the dark night, she linked up with four hooded men who led her to an almost inaccessible cove where a launch was waiting. Using the oars for silence, they began the journey to Alderney. After one mile, they put a spurt on, using the engine until nearing the shores of their destination, where once again, rowing with the oars, they pulled into the discreet cove, marked previously by Cassie. Guiding the men, as near to the huts as was safe, they hid in some bushes. The sound of machinery and slight explosions nearby made her heart sink. What if he was working and not in the hut? Number fifty six, the thought struck her like a mallet.

Soldiers, on guard duty, marched backwards and forwards before the huts, she could just about see the glint of their bayonets. The pressure was building up. What if this, what if that? The waiting unbearable. Before she could ply her mind further, one of the Resistance sprang silently from the bush. She heard a gurgle and then silence. Daring to look, a soldier lay motionless on the ground. Within seconds, the second guard was finished off and they turned their attention to the huts. Despite the expediency of the occasion, a cold shiver ran through her at the taking of life. In no time, one of the Resistance, a skilled locksmith was scouting the huts for the correct number. It was pitch-black, Cassie dare not shift from her position, she longed to delve the huts with the man. After what seemed hours, though it could not have been more than a few minutes, a faint shadow emerged from the shacks. He appeared to be carrying something but had yet to cross open country. A searchlight ringed the compound and at its passing, two of the hooded men slipped silently from their hiding place, to the assistance of their man, who, to escape the beams of the searchlight, had thrown himself and the rescued Georges to the ground. Cassie knew little else; she was in such a state of fear and jubilation. A rough hand on her shoulder warned her that they were moving out. Carrying Georges between them they made for the cove. Almost nearing their goal, the sound of singing soldiers came towards them. Slipping back into the hedge, two soldiers passed them, possibly the changing of guard. Immediately, two of the Resistance, silently and swiftly, felled them to the ground and hid them in the bushes, the same as they had done to the previous two. It would have been fatal for them to have sounded the alarm.

Cassie, this time, was too much on edge to be concerned. Descending the high cliff with Georges was tricky, weak and ill as he was. Once on the launch, she nestled him like a baby. It could be seen that, without attention, he would not last much longer. With her face blacked it would have been difficult to recognise her; if he did, he showed little response. All was quiet above. Digging the oars, they sailed smoothly towards the open sea and without any further mishap brought the launch into their secret lair. Leaving two men to return the borrowed launch, they were hoisted up into the cave. She cleansed her face, between washing his poor, starved, festered body and raised him in her arms to give him nourishment. His face broke into a wonderful smile and his lips called her name. With tears streaming their cheeks, they lay overwhelmed by the outpouring of blinding love, so wonderful it could not be spent. It was not for them to fathom out the next step.

Linked up to Whitehall in London, the resistance received the joyful news that a submarine would, in two days time, make its appearance and take them back to England.

The following two days were tortuous to Cassie. Georges was getting weaker, he needed urgent medical assistance. Nearer the time, she scanned the waters and thanked God for a calm night. One of the resistance would accompany them to England. She longed for them to reveal themselves with the mistaken belief that her grateful thanks would be more fully received.

She could not believe her eyes when lowered from the cave she landed into the wherry. Her companion whom she called Jack laughed heartily but said nothing. Seated in the wherry with her beloved Georges in her arms she waited for those above to spy the submarine. The signal given, her companion took the oars. Eventually, they saw a long grey blob and excitedly made their way towards it. Drawing nearer they could see the outlines of the submarine. Cassie felt quite elated. A bright light almost blinded her. In her innocence, she thought it had come from the submarine to assist their passage.

"Down," yelled her companion.

The searchlight continued to hold the little boat in its grip. Bullets came thick and fast. Bending low, shielding her sick husband as well as she could, she envisaged the end of them all. Daring to look up, she saw the oarsman slumped across his seat, blood spurting his mouth. Open mouthed, she gently let go of Georges and automatically took the oars and rowed, where, she did not know. The submarine had, oh, so unkindly disappeared.

Alone, destitute of light of any kind, the calm, untroubled waters only seemed to emphasise her plight. Feeling beyond the point where she could help herself, she took Georges once again into her arms. The wherry, lost without its navigator, bobbed and turned. She took the lifeless, oarsman's hand, it was cold, she rubbed it.

"We shall be together, I thank you."

A sudden rush of water nearly turned the boat. Looking up, she witnessed the emergence of a grey shadow only a few yards distance. Desperate, she rowed towards it and in a short time the three of them were safely aboard the submarine and on their way to England. From the comfort of the bunk where she had been laid she could see her unknown, fellow traveller receiving attention. His balaclava was off and they were trying to stem the flow of blood. He was a most dreadful colour. Her body shook. It was Reine. She thought when he spoke on the wherry that his voice sounded familiar but the situation had been too fraught.

Warmth, food and loving care did wonders for Georges. He rallied a little of his old self and Cassie thought it safe to tell him of Reine. In a quiet way, she told him of his adventurous, protective spirit during dangerous times. He was a man of courage to the end. She wheeled him to his dead friend's side and left them awhile.

Returning, she knew by the expression on Georges face that it had been the right thing.

Overjoyed at returning to England with Georges, Cassie could almost have kissed the ground. A couple of rooms in the East End with Georges, overlooking the river, fulfilled her every wish. He would soon be well. Sometimes, he would rally round, talk and take an interest in the river traffic. They would laugh at the vibrant conversations echoing around the streets; so normal for Cassie, so novel to Georges. At other times, he was content just to lie and hold Cassie's hand.

One morning, Cassie woke to find Georges feeling unusually still by her side. Holding him tightly in her arms, she pressed her warm face against his cold cheeks.

"Darling, you're freezing. I'll warm you."

"Have a little sleep, then we will walk the river."

An eerie silence encompassed the room.

Sam stood at the door speaking softly, "Ge' 'er aaht, gel."

Sarah gently prised her daughter away.

"Don't wake him, he's tired. Sleep well darling. It's high tide; we'll have a jaunt in the Caroline." She laughed and left the room.

A haunting mist hung the river. The Caroline, bruised but not beaten, chafed against its shackles. With arms outstretched the mist surrounded her like a shroud, enveloping her ill clad body.

"Georges, Georges, wait for me, I'm coming." Her voice carried the waters and was lost in the aqueous vapours of time.

East End Glossary

'Aves - Haves
'Eard - Heard

A gate - Mouth
Aaht (aht) - Out
Abaht - About
Accant (accahnt) - Account
Ah (aah) - Our
Ahses - Houses

Baize - Coarse woollen cloth
Blue Rinse - Blue powder used for washing clothes to make whites look whiter
Bolster - Large pillow going full width of bed
Bonse - Head
Borrer - Borrow
Brick dust scour - Used to sharpen and polish knives

Cah - Cow
Carpet Beater - A wicker bat shaped article used to beat the dust out of mats
Cawled - Called
Cobbling - Shoe mending
Cock up - Mess up

Drahned - Drowned

Gel - Girl
Git - Get
Golden Balls - Horse dung

Haudasity - Audacity
Hawser - Small cable

Lighter - Large flat bottomed boats for loading and unloading ships
Lightermen - Men who worked the large flat bottomed boats
Long run and Fell - Type of stitching
Longuns - Long trousers

M'athed - Mouthed
Mahth - Mouth (exaggerated)

Naah (nah) - Now
Nowt - Nothing

One and sixpence - Equivalent to 7p
Owf - Off

Paff - Path
Pahned - Pound
Pinny - Apron
Poe - Chamber pot

Raahnd (rahned) - Round
Rubbing board - Board used to rub clothes to wash them clean

Shilling - Equivalent to 5p
Sloop - A vessel with one mast, hardly different from a cutler

The'd - They'd
Threehapence - Equivalent to less than 1p
Thre'pence - Equivalent to 1p
Trahsers - Trousers
Tuppence - Two old pennies

Watcha cock - A hello greeting
Withaaht - Without

Ya, (yer) - you
Yella - Yellow
Yer've - You have